Among Lions

Books by J. Allan Bosworth

FOR YOUNG PEOPLE

A BIRD FOR PETER
VOICES IN THE MEADOW
WHITE WATER, STILL WATER
ALL THE DARK PLACES
A WIND NAMED ANNE
A DARKNESS OF GIANTS
AMONG LIONS

NOVELS

SPEED DEMON
THE LONG WAY NORTH

Among Lions

BY J. ALLAN BOSWORTH

1973

Doubleday & Company, Inc., Garden City, New York

. . . my soul is among lions.

     —The Book of
     Common Prayer

Among Lions

1.

Jesse Seward watched the Jeep until its tail light was only a feeble red spark. And when the light winked out and was gone, he clung to the faint reports of the engine's exhaust until it, too, was lost. Only then, when the cool smell of settling dust was all that remained, did he finally move and go back to the wagon. Climbing to its high seat, he did not yet turn the old horse from its rest, but waited, still feeling that he had wandered into the webs of a nightmare. And whose dream was it, his father's or his own? A dream in which Virgil Seward had become a stranger, and some kind of malignant shadow darkened a once-familiar earth. . . .

This place, high in the Sierra's western slopes, belonged to Charlie and Martha Fergus. So did the Jeep, and that clattering relic of an old war was the only means of getting Virgil down to the nearest road, and from there, across the miles to a hospital.

Jesse still trembled with it, the fright of his trip here in the wagon. His father had collapsed that afternoon, and during four jolting miles had lost consciousness . . . like a man slowly bleeding to death. Martha was an ex-nurse, and in her loud, red-headed way, she assured him that it was probably just exhaustion and his old stomach trouble flaring up . . . nothing to be alarmed about. But within a very few minutes, she and Charlie had him in the Jeep and were gone. And now, night was coming. . . .

Their hired hand watched from near the house, and the sadness of what he did not understand made a hang-dog shadow of him. Joe was perhaps thirty now, strong and a good worker at simple tasks. But his eyes, his few words and quick way of laughing were those of a man unaware that, in his mind, he would never be older than twelve. Jesse thought to speak, but then the man seemed suddenly aware of the darkness and hurried, limping, inside . . . and this too was part of the night-mare. Trying not to think about it, Jesse slapped the reins across the horse's rump. Home now—if it was home.

He gave the horse its head; it knew that faintly rutted path far better than he did. *Home,* he wondered—how could it be questioned? It or the man who lived there? But he had not seen his father or that house for eleven years. Not until three days ago. And returning then, what had he found?

Jesse slumped on the seat and watched the passing dark caverns of trees, and let his mind drift. . .

Virgil retreated to the Sierra Nevada twenty-three years ago, a fugitive from the frantic postwar boom that had turned his beloved California into a circus of change. Going high into the slopes where not many others were likely to follow, he bought a section of land and spent the next three years building a world more to his liking.

Camping on a level knoll with an old tractor and a belt-driven saw, he cut timber to raise a house and a barn, and broke the earth for planting. He enclosed and divided the rest of his square mile with fences, and stocked it with a few head of cattle and sheep, and two horses. And when it was done, Virgil went back to San Francisco to marry Jessica and bring her home. Then, in 1953, a son . . .

It was a hidden kind of existence—one that, in many ways, belonged to another time. There was no electricity and no telephone, and no mail or news except when they went to Dardanelle once a month. And yet Jesse remembered it as being good. In that sturdy house, and in the warmth of themselves, they were a happy sufficiency against all the wilderness around them.

But after a while, somehow, it was lost. Maybe that kind of life was only for the young and foolish, and maybe isolation was a slow disease. Whatever the reason, a brittleness came to Jessica. It did not matter that they had acquired neighbors only four miles away, and the monthly trip to Dardanelle was not enough. She was lonely for lights, noise, the ceaseless vitality of a city. And too, she complained more and more about not being able to teach Jesse enough; he needed a school and real teachers, and he needed to be around other kids.

Virgil had no answers to any of it. He could not stop her loneliness, and there was not money enough to board Jesse in Dardanelle, and he did not know how to turn away and leave his square-mile world.

Jesse was only eight when it happened. His mother had left her bed in the dark of a Sunday morning to come to his room and whisper him awake. He remembered staring at the two suitcases while Jessica quietly urged him into his clothes, and then being led half asleep out to the barn. They were going on a trip, that was all she would say, and although she had not done it before, that small woman somehow managed to harness the horse and hitch it to the wagon. They drove away through dawn and sunrise, reaching the Ferguses in time to catch a ride into Dardanelle, where Charlie and Martha attended church. From there, because she did not have much money, it became a grasshopper's journey from truckstop to truckstop, sometimes waiting for hours in those steamy roadside restaurants before Jessica could find a trucker to take them on down the road. It was a day and a half before, tired and dirty, they stood at the foot of Market Street in San Francisco.

Pointing into that noisy, vibrant confusion, Jessica told the boy, "This is home . . . your real home."

Eleven years later, he had to carry her out of her small, Russian Hill apartment and rush to a hospital. Within a few short days, she was dead.

With the jolting of the wagon, he found the trees again, shadows in a surrounding black. Jesse did not want to think about the funeral, or that week of aimless, empty wandering around San Francisco before deciding to come back here. And he was not really sure why he had returned. Once it had been a matter of being too young to travel alone, and for a time money was the problem. After a while, even the letters stopped; Virgil was almost inarticulate when it came to scrawling words on paper. But, for all those years, Jesse had been growing and changing; this became the real distance between them, and a kind that was difficult to cross.

Jesse knew he had not come back because of his mother; he was old enough to be alone. Curiosity, perhaps, or some faint remnant of obligation; and maybe, before he could truly be on his own, he had to repair that broken connection with the past. Such things were only guesses. But he had returned—and to what?

It was not a remembered home; the house seemed smaller now, and huddled in a chill of unnamed differences. And the man who lived there—like a reflection in a distorting mirror, he was only vaguely familiar and therefore disturbing. When he first came, it was a shock to find a short, gray, and balding man. He had, of course, last seen his father from the standpoint of a child, and a man's aging, left unobserved for a time, always seemed more obvious. Too, Virgil's disconcerting spells of pain kept pushing him even farther out of reach. But these things were on the surface and at least within comprehension. If like a reflection, there was more moving within the dark of the glass . . .

Virgil, too, could not quite grasp the fact of his own kin. But it was not just the estrangement and awkwardness of too many years. And neither was it a question of a face having been lost. With his reddish hair, green eyes, and slender features, Jesse was an unmistakable echo of his mother; Virgil knew who it was before he reached the house. The veil between them was something else, and at first, Jesse knew only that it had to do with the mountains towering above the house—something that festered and tore at Virgil's mind.

The man had taken to sleeping by day and pacing at night . . . pacing, or sitting woodenly and staring at the walls as if, through them, he could see the mountains. Jesse had wondered if his father had simply lived alone too long; certainly the ravages of deep isolation were obvious in his eyes and his way of talking. And on the second night, the festering had broken loose, Virgil twisting his fingers into Jesse's arm and pointing wild-eyed toward those star-searching ridges. He whispered almost incoherently of an image from hell, and then fell into a brooding silence.

Not until last night had Virgil given it a name. One of the dogs barked, and it did not strike Jesse as being important; dogs were inclined to challenge the dark at times. But Virgil let out a curse and ran to the back porch to fire his rifle into the blackness. And at what? There was nothing to be seen or heard, and yet he emptied the rifle . . . fired the last shot, and as if in a helpless rage, smashed the weapon against a porch stanchion. Jesse questioned him several times before Virgil was coherent enough to speak.

"*Lion*," he said, and that was all. But he had uttered the word as if it were not quite enough.

Lion . . . and with it identified, Jesse still had wondered. While they were an endangered species, now, the creatures were not a surprising or unexpected part of the Sierras. And though the cats took a sheep or a calf now and then, they could not really be considered a problem, not to the extent suggested by Virgil's behavior. It was more reasonable to believe that, being ill, he had reacted to something that existed only in delirium. But this evening, when Martha looked down at

Virgil's unconscious form, she had shaken her head and murmured, "Lord knows we've all been afraid. But he's had it worse, being alone. . . . Jesse, you stay inside at night. Understand?"

2.

Jesse freed the horse and stood in the dark of the barn, staring at the house. It was not easy, giving up four miles and coming back, and those last few yards were the worst. Had he begun to know his father again, or if he had returned in the simple light of day, he might have grasped some small, familiar thing to make a difference. But the house, that supposed root of his life, seemed locked in night and made of brooding.

He did not know how to measure Martha's warning to stay in at night. Maybe it was one thing for Virgil, in the crush of solitude, to take the ordinary and twist it into frightened exaggeration. But the Ferguses had each other, and they even had a hired hand for added company. But Joe was an unwanted thought, and rather than consider his part in the nightmare, Jesse impulsively crossed that star-covered space. The lamps were all he could think of, now, as if, in their glow, he could escape what he felt. And if he escaped, sleep was the shortest distance to morning.

He went to each lamp in the house, and the lighting of them was a ritual against the night. And when their glowing filled the rooms, Jesse perched on the edge of a chair and tried to know the difference they made. Silence overwhelmed it all; there were no crickets yet, to touch those chill spring nights. Seeing the old Victrola in the corner, he hurried to it and cranked it up. There was a record already on the turntable, covered with years of dust. He blew it away . . . Debussy. It must have been Jessica's. The idea wrenched at him, but he settled the needle into the groove and wandered away, listening to the thin, scratchy remains of an orchestra.

So old, far away . . . not just the music, but that room, the whole house. More and more, he knew a sense of distance yawning between him and what, once, was home. It did not matter, what Martha had said. He wondered if his father would be back, and wished now that he had asked to squeeze into the Jeep and go with them to where there were electric lights, and sounds, and people. Returning here made no sense, now, except that something was trying to die, some faintly remembered part of himself.

The Victrola needed winding, but not listening, he went to his room and stretched out on the bed. It had been a long day and a bad one, reason enough to be tired and tired enough to sleep. Still, he could do no more than close his eyes, and when he did, he saw everything happening again. Virgil collapsing, the long trip in the wagon, his father passing out and the pale look of dying in his face . . . the Jeep roaring off . . . yes, and Joe hurrying, limping, to get away from the dark . . . and himself . . . what was he but a spectator among strangers, a visitor in a bad dream?

If there was any chance for sleep, it was quickly lost. Somewhere on the slope above the house, a scream tore at the dark. Jesse sat up and froze as the dogs sounded the alarm. Beneath their frenzied bugling, he soon heard a disturbance among the sheep. The lion—it had come down from the mountains.

He had no idea of what could be done, but sounds of agony jarred him into motion. Finding the big six-cell flashlight, he ran outside and to the far corner of the barn. Near the end of the light's reach, the sheep were barely visible; he could see them, and the dogs working to keep them together. Not finding any sign of a lion, but cautious and afraid, Jesse went up the slope until he could just see the back fence and its wide, wooden gate. From there, he carefully probed with the light again. It revealed the dead sheep this time, and another was kicking its last a few yards to the left. But the expected image did not present itself.

Nothing was somehow worse than something. Terribly aware of the distance to the house, he turned and ran. It was a swift and mindless thing, aiming for lighted windows with all the dark pressing against his back; and somewhere toward the last, not far from the door, he felt a different air—a stirring of it, like breath, and warm. Spinning around and ready to scream, Jesse stabbed at the night with a bright beam. And he was quite alone.

Jesse pushed into the kitchen, locked the door, and stood there trembling. That moment of *feeling* the lion's presence, and turning to find nothing—it was a sharp reminder of what had happened to Joe. That unfortunate soul had walked out to the barn at the Ferguses a few weeks ago, and though the moon was full, unknowingly cornered the lion. In breaking free, the cat knocked him down and clawed one leg rather badly. But afterward,

Joe babbled about a ghost and insisted that he had seen nothing.

Retreating to the front room, Jesse sat down and wondered where his good sense had gone. Tonight, the lion *had* come. It screamed, the dogs reacted, and two sheep were dead. This was reality, and he had not seen the lion because it had seen him first, and associating man with rifles, slipped off into the dark beyond the fence. It was that simple. The rest was only imagined.

But, for all his reasoning, he still could not relax. He was safe inside, and so it was not a matter of being afraid that the lion might return before light to claim one of its kills. Indeed, he wondered if it was important. The damage, for that night, had been done. It was, instead, a suspicion of futility that agitated at the back of his mind, a feeling that the lion was somehow immune to anything that might be tried against it.

Although the notion was absurd, he could not dismiss it entirely. And he was not ignoring his own susceptibility. The Ferguses were unsettling with their apparent readiness to call the lion supernatural. And he could not have remained untouched by the ravings of a father he no longer knew. But at the core of absurdity was a fact for which he saw no reasonable explanation. Martha had told him, and his own experience had given her words an unexpected emphasis.

The fact was that, although sheep and calves had been lost to it, no one had ever seen the lion. And maybe that was understandable up to a point. No doubt it was very clever to make its kills at the far edge of a pasture, and very wise to react quickly to the first signs of having been discovered. But for it to *always* escape a flashlight's beam was hard to accept. And Joe, who had come into actual contact . . . even allowing for his limited mind, how could he have not seen at least *something?* Moreover, back in the beginning, Charlie and Virgil had tried several times to hunt it down in broad daylight, but not once had they found tracks that did not, sooner or later, fade into nothing.

Supernatural? Jesse groaned and still refused. The lion was flesh and blood; it had to be. But there seemed to be no way of coming to grips with it.

The pattern would continue, he knew. Seemingly invisible, the cat would always come down from the mountains, looking to have its way with the poor beasts within his father's fences. *Always?* It sounded immortal, and might as well have been. With Virgil gone, his rifle silenced, what reason would the lion have to even hesitate? A few dogs, a flashlight . . . maybe, he thought bitterly, a toy gun tucked away somewhere in the gatherings of his childhood.

Sooner or later the lion would know the rifle was gone, and having less to fear of a man and a light, would retreat not to leave but to wait. The dogs were the best of what was left, and not enough—not in the dark with a flock of fear-crazed sheep.

Toy . . . something shifted in his mind and clamored across the years. But Jesse slipped away from it, staring at that room. No way of coming to grips; if his father came back, it would all begin again. A man he did not know, caught in an apparently futile struggle with something that, strangely, had yet to be seen. And this house, what was left of home, would go on drifting, backward and backward, until it was beyond retrieving. Maybe it

had already passed out of reach, and he wondered if
it would not be best to walk to the Ferguses in the morning. They might be back by then, and could take him to
the bus. With its bay and gentle hills, San Francisco
was at least something he knew and understood.

Yes, maybe . . . but for now, silence and the long reach
of night. Knowing he still could not sleep, Jesse went to
the small collection of books that filled a shelf near the
fireplace. Except for a few volumes on animal diseases,
most had belonged to Jessica. The copy of *The Yearling*
was his. And three Oz books . . . he had forgotten about
them, and picked one up to start thumbing through it.
Maybe it was this connection with childhood that trig-
gered it, but that clamoring came again. Toy . . . yellow box . . .

Putting the book back, Jesse returned to the chair. Why
a yellow box? And if there was a toy rifle somewhere,
what difference did it make? The lion was not one of
childhood's beasts to be magically slain by a popping
cork. But still . . . something was trying to come together, fragments rising to the surface . . . yellow
box . . . toy, the thin touch of oil . . .

Annoyed and curious, he went to his bedroom. The
closet was a likely place. It was jammed with old clothes
and those he had brought from the city, but not until
now had he thought to see what else might be stored
there. Pushing the clothes aside and peering into that
dim space, he saw a large box and something leaning in
the corner. Jesse pulled both into the light and soon
learned that he had not found any answers. It was merely
a fishing pole, and the assorted junk that only a small
boy could treasure.

He put them back, and tried to make sense of what the faint shards of memory were trying to tell him . . . the barn, tool shed . . . or a darker place that belonged to someone else . . . a small boy had been attracted to it.

On a hunch, and not caring to go outside, Jesse went to his father's cluttered room. Glancing around, he again decided that a closet was the best place. Some of Jessica's dresses were there, and Virgil's threadbare Sunday suit. The floor was lost under shoes, boots, and dirty laundry, and Jesse wondered if there was any point in going on. The changes that had taken place since Jessica left were more obvious in that room than anywhere else. It did not seem likely that what he was trying to recall could still be there . . . if it ever was. But those dresses, the suit—something about them bothered him. Reaching past the clothes, he felt a round hatbox, the back wall; and then, in the corner, cool oiled metal—the barrel of a rifle.

Jesse got it out and saw that it was a .30-30 lever-action carbine. And attached to the lever was a tag that read, "For Jesse on his twelfth birthday." With that, it all came back, and he knew why he had thought of a toy. Like the fathers who bought boxing gloves for their baby sons, Virgil had bought him a rifle and put it away until he was big enough. Jesse supposed he had found the gun when he was too young to know it was real. Probably he was caught, scolded, and told to stay out of the closet. And toys that had to wait were, sooner or later, forgotten.

Finding the cartridges, twenty in a yellow box, Jesse took the rifle to the front room. After cleaning the carbine with a handkerchief and removing the tag, he loaded it and sighted along the barrel. The first thought was that he could build a blind on the slope and wait for the lion. But he realized how awkward it would be to aim both rifle and flashlight, and what little chance there was of the cat coming over the fence in exactly the right place. He would have to be free to move around, but then the lion would see him. No, he decided, about the best he could do was go out and fire it into the air when the dogs sounded the alarm. It was no more than his father had done the night he smashed the big rifle, but at least no sheep had died then. And so, except for the noise it made, the carbine was still no better than a toy.

When dawn came and grew old enough for seeing, Jesse took the carbine outside, wanting nothing more than to hear the noise it made. He took careful aim at a fence post and pulled the trigger. With that sudden explosion, chunks of wood flew from the post. Startled by the power he held in his hands, he fired again . . . and something came into focus—something he perhaps had not dared consider in the dark of a long night. But with the echoes still cascading down, he looked up at the high and far reaches of the Sierra Nevada, and knew that he would hunt the lion.

3.

It was an odd feeling to stand aside, in a sense, and quarrel with this view of himself preparing for four or five days in the mountains. The question was not that of getting lost or starving. He had gone camping with his San Francisco friends a few times, and he knew the requirements. Neither was it a matter of not being able to put the rifle to good use should the occasion arise. With those same boys, he had done enough target shooting to become a passable marksman. And although it was easy to be brave in the bright sun of morning, it certainly was not a matter of giving in to any notion that the lion was supernatural. It was just that he had never gone hunting before, and the idea of going after a mountain lion struck him as being nothing less than preposterous.

What hope did he have? There was a lot of big, hard country between the slopes of home and those high, remote battlements where snow defied the season. And somewhere in it all, a big cat—a creature that could move like smoke and vanish just as easily. What hope, indeed. The whole thing was intimidating, to say the least, and he paused in his preparations to remind himself that it was not too late to change his mind.

But Jesse looked around at the dimming fact of what once was home, and knew he could not leave it—not yet. And neither could he stay there and do nothing. The chance, however small, had to be taken.

The last item on the list was the flashlight. He remembered leaving it on the kitchen table, last night, after coming in from the slope. And going to get it, now, he found that the batteries were dead. In his fright, he had stood it on end, lens down, without thinking to turn it off.

Disgusted, Jesse spent a few minutes looking for extra batteries, and failed to find them. He supposed it was not important. There was no intention, at least, of traveling or trying to hunt after dark. And when he was camped at night, he would always have a fire anyway.

After carrying everything outside, he went into the barn and located two burlap bags and a piece of canvas. The bags would hold the supplies, and combined with blankets, the canvas would make a bedroll. Looking at it all, Jesse was satisfied that he had not exceeded necessity; it was enough to sustain him without burdening the horse and slowing them down.

"What you do?"

Startled by the voice, Jesse turned and saw that it was Joe. "What are you doing here? Have the Ferguses come back?"

Joe blinked. "No."

"Then you don't know how my father is," Jesse said the obvious, and bent to start loading the burlap bags.

"Sick," Joe told him.

"Yes."

"What you do, Mr. Jesse?"

"I'm going after the lion."

Joe flinched and looked all around them, as if the very mention of the cat were dangerous. Then, half smiling, he said, "You won't get him."

"Probably not. But it doesn't hurt to try."

"Ghost."

"No, Joe, it isn't a ghost. Just smart, that's all."

Joe pulled up his pants leg to reveal the long, pink furrow of a new scar. "He done it to me, Mr. Jesse, and I didn't see nothin'!"

There was no use in arguing with the man; that simple mind grasped an idea with the faith of a child and was not easily changed. "Tell you what, Joe. While I'm doing this, why don't you go get the sorrel for me. See him out there?" Jesse pointed at the lower pasture north of the house.

By the time Joe found a hackamore in the barn, walked out to the pasture, and brought the sorrel in, Jesse had all his supplies divided equally between the two bags and ready to go. After he lashed the bedroll into a hard, tight cylinder, he went to get a small saddle that must have been his a long time ago. This, with its blanket, he put on the horse.

Joe thought it was very funny. "Too little! Your knees bump your ears!"

Jesse grinned at him. "I won't be riding. This is just to hang the bags on." He suspended the bags from the saddle horn so that they hung evenly on both sides of the horse. "See?"

He tied the bedroll behind the saddle and, with that,

was ready to leave. Cradling the carbine in the crook
of his arm, he turned to Joe and said, "You better go
home. But listen, see to it that somebody comes and
feeds the dogs. Okay?"

"Okay Mr. Jesse. But you ain't going to get him."

"We'll see."

Jesse led the sorrel up across the slope where the
sheep were, and heading for the upper gate, passed close
to the two that were killed last night. He stopped for a
moment, surprised to see that there was no blood on the
carcasses. Their backs had been broken, of course, but
it was almost easy to look at unmarked bodies and think
in terms of something unreal—as if mere shadows could
kill. Uncomfortable with a feeling that should not have
survived the night, he went on to the gate, and beyond
that fence, aimed for those higher places.

It was a slow pace, one that gave little disturbance
to the countryside around them. He knew better than
to think that the lion could not detect their presence
from a long distance away, but he wondered if being
unhurried would not tend to disguise his intentions and
perhaps make the lion less wary. Too, he climbed slowly
rather than tax the old horse or himself more than was
necessary. The land was as yet comparatively gentle in
its rising. It had to break across a number of lesser crests
before meeting the last high ridge and those final mas-
sifs, the icy towers that reached for world's end. But he
still found himself stopping frequently to rest. San Francisco had given him legs for hills, but not lungs for pro-
longed climbing.

What bothered him most, though, was the aimlessness
he felt. Jesse remained alert to his surroundings, watch-

ing for tracks and any hint of motion in the rocks and trees around him. And yet it seemed to him that there had to be more to hunting than that, and he wished he could have talked to somebody before starting out. Confronted with a huge expanse of God's creation, there had to be some kind of choice—one based on logic, which in turn was based on a lion's habits.

It was obvious, even to Jesse, that a lion would spend most of its time on the prowl. And, as would follow, *where* it was would be determined by the location and numbers of other animals. The latter, he supposed, moved according to the season and the weather—how wet it was, or dry, and how warm or cold.

But what about a lion that acquired a taste for man's sheep and cattle? If driven to it by winter, winter was gone . . . and so where were the usual patterns of its kind?

The only hopeful thing about it that Jesse could see was that this lion would not be ranging as far as would otherwise be the case. It had to be there, somewhere, between home and the snow. Indeed, considering the frequency of its visits, the lion's den was probably well below those wintry summits. But what a small and dismal hope it was! No matter how much it could be narrowed down by probability, it was still a massive landscape, one in which, several times, Charlie and Virgil had hunted the lion and failed. A lion, Jesse reminded himself, that had managed to hide in the small nightshadows of a barn, and escape the eyes of the man it mauled.

Perhaps, then, he was doing all that could be done, which was to move across that terrain and search for some kind of clue. But if that was the best, it was not encouraging.

Encountering nothing more than a deer, which watched without concern from a distance of three hundred yards, Jesse reached the third ridge by noon. Feeling hot and shaky, and realizing he had not eaten since yesterday, he staked the horse out to graze and hurriedly fixed a cold meal. Wolfing it down to get some sugar back into his system, he berated himself for his foolishness. The altitude there was not much, somewhere between four thousand and five thousand feet. But one still did not climb with an empty stomach, for long, without paying the price.

And the second mistake was to remain there for a while after eating. A full stomach combined with a sleepless night, and he soon had no choice but to stretch out in the shade of a tree and drowse for an hour or two.

It was late afternoon when he stirred. The sun had found his eyes, and he rolled over, groaning, to lie on his stomach. Were it not for the time lost, he might have given in and slept some more. But there had to be more to show for that day; he had yet to go very far, and though there was nothing yet to follow, it seemed important to get higher before the sun went down.

Jesse's mind was still in a fog when he sat up. He had slept too hard, and for too short a time. Wetting his hands with the canteen, he rubbed his face and felt the water turn cold in the light breeze that had come up. He watched the horse grazing, for a moment. Then, as if trying to summon the will to move, he stared upward toward the next ridge—and saw the lion.

It was standing motionless, there in a dark stand of pine. Had there been no sun to catch its eyes and the white around its jaw and neck, it would have been no more than a shadow and probably missed. Slow to react, Jesse turned to find his rifle. And when he looked back, there was nothing . . . only the trees. Only a matter of seconds . . . there, and not there. An illusion?

Quickly, he slung the bags on the saddle horn, and took the sorrel with him rather than leave it unprotected. Crossing that distance, Jesse realized it would have been foolish to try a shot. Very probably he would have missed or only wounded the animal, and either way, the lion would have been warned of his intentions. But even so, he was disappointed with his response to the encounter. It was too slow and disorganized. He had been caught off guard, and no doubt there would be few enough opportunities without wasting them.

Reaching the trees and tying the sorrel, Jesse searched the immediate area. The lion was gone, of course. But studying the needle-covered ground beneath the trees, and then moving around the perimeter of that stand, he could not even find a single track to indicate that a lion had ever been there. Spirit . . . fragment of his own mind . . . it was a temptation to give in to such thoughts, but he preferred to think that the ground was too hard. And, considering the broad, soft pads of its feet and the way a cat walked, he supposed there was no reason why there had to be a visible disturbance in that carpet of dry pine needles. Most likely of all, he probably just did not know how to read the ground for such signs.

But then, only a few feet away from him, a rabbit broke cover and ran. Why, he wondered, had it not run before?

And why was the horse not snorting and acting up at some lingering scent? It was this, rather than the absence of any visible trace, that sent something prickling across his spine.

There was nothing to be done except to push such questions away and go on. If there had been anything, that day, there was nothing more. Only a deep quiet and a coming dark.

4.

The sun went down early in the mountains, and warned by the beginnings of twilight, Jesse continued only for the little time it took to reach a grassy knoll. Putting the horse on a long tether for grazing, he made several quick trips to the nearest stand of trees and collected enough wood to last the night. Then, near the edge of what would be the sorrel's turning, he made a ring of stones and there built his fire.

It was comforting, that brightness and cheery crackling. But Jesse looked beyond it and questioned the value of the day just over. In trying to deal with the lion he had only just begun, really, and now he had been stopped again.

Night, he supposed, was the hunter's frustration. Robbed by evolution of those very senses that gave an animal the freedom of the dark, man could only wait, imprisoned, until light returned. He did not begrudge any animal the few advantages it might hold over those who hunted in the dubious name of sport. But what of necessity? Although it no doubt helped to be a good hunter, it seemed to him a discouraging inequity in which all the gains of a day were too easily canceled by the mere setting of the sun.

Too tired to brood about it for long, Jesse cooked a simple meal of bacon and beans, and then crawled into his bedroll. And it was good to stretch out, to feel the grass-softened ground beneath him and watch with half-closed eyes the broad sweep of the Milky Way. But in spite of that exhausting and unaccustomed day, sleep was elusive.

His muscles conspired against him, jumping now and then as if discharging some kind of electricity. But even when that part of him settled down, something in his mind refused to let go. Perhaps he was still too accustomed to nights filled with the sounds of a city, not this high, wind-singing silence. And so he drifted, neither asleep nor awake.

San Francisco: a place of pigeons and bells, Italians, cable cars clanging up Powell Street . . . Chinese New Year, a time of firecrackers and smoke, and twisting, many-legged dragons . . . and his mother . . . the warm years on Russian Hill . . . books, music, walks on the beach and happy dinners together . . . and yet a certain loneliness for both of them. Maybe that was why they kept so busy . . . yes, and then so suddenly and quickly, Jessica was gone. The emergency ward, a few days in a private room, and that was it. He had gone home from the hospital, and unable to stay in those rooms, went walking in the night and the fog. And he had gotten as far as Stanyan Street before he cried.

The past slowly moved off into the dark and was lost, and this time of wind and stars grew dim. With the fire burning low, he was finally close to sleep. But there on

the soft edges of unknowing peace, something intruded
to make him jerk and come sharply awake. Perhaps it
was no more than the beginning of a dream, or the ending of some unnoticed reality, but part of that wind was
not wind—something was out of harmony with its sound.
And beyond the dying fire, somewhere in the black, a
brief hint of motion . . . there, and just as quickly, not
there.

Jesse sat up, and trying to be quiet about it, slowly
worked the carbine's lever to put a cartridge in the
chamber. In the cold, brittle air, even that smooth, oiled
mechanism sounded harsh and loud; surely the wind carried the noise to betray him. But he lowered the hammer
to the safety position and waited, straining at the dark
and trying to hear something smaller than the wind
and the voice of pines. And what was he trying to hear?
Grass being bent, the stirring of a pebble? He might as
well have been listening for a fish swimming at the
bottom of a deep pool, when there was no certainty that
a fish was even near.

For nearly an hour, moving only to turn his head, he
gave it every chance to happen again. But whatever it
was, if it was anything, had gone. The lion? He shud-
dered, and aware now of how thoroughly the cold had
crept into his bones, he built the fire up again. If it was
the lion, he thought, then what had it wanted? What
would have happened if he had gone on sleeping by
a dying fire? Probably nothing. Maybe it was only the
dark that made it an uncomfortable idea.

As soon as he was warm, Jesse went back to his blankets. But he propped himself up on his elbows, still too
full of wondering. Maybe it was only a deer accustomed

to grazing on that knoll at night, or passing that way headed for water. Or it could have been a fox or bobcat; certainly the lion was not the only animal living in those parts. The problem, though, was in knowing which was which. It would be silly to lose sleep, jumping at everything that moved or made a sound. He wished almost angrily that he had the flashlight, but then realized that if it was the lion, the light probably would only drive it farther into the mountains. For now at least, there was still a possibility that the cat regarded him with curiosity rather than as a threat.

He supposed that, if he ever managed to find tracks and started following them, it was inevitable that the lion would catch on to his game. And then, Jesse imagined, the cat would do everything to throw him off. Very probably it would succeed, and unless he was very lucky, that would be the end of the hunt.

It might have helped to have at least a general idea of where the lion went after its raids. Then he could have looked for a cave, or a sheltering overhang of rock—anything a lion might use for a den. But, according to Charlie and Virgil, the big cat's traces just faded out, came to nothing, as if the animal simply ceased to exist. The worst of such nonsense was that his own experience, that day, seemed to support it.

Jesse wished that he could have been sure of his own senses—convinced that what he saw was real, or certain that it was no more than an expected image planted in his mind by his father and the Ferguses. All that business of the supernatural . . .

Maybe being away from the house and alone—especially now, in the dark—he was, in spite of himself, giving it too much importance. But from what little he did know about mountain lions, Jesse could not help being aware of a difference. There was that question of why it raided livestock, for one thing. It made sense during a hard winter, but why in the spring, when the mountains were alive with game? And the night Joe unwittingly cornered it by the barn—why was the lion there, so close? It seemed so unlikely that the cat could have been so slow in detecting a man's approach, or be so easily boxed in. The only answer that made any sense at all was an unusual boldness—this when mountain lions were known for their timidity toward man. The lion had run, of course, from rifle shots and the beam of a flashlight, and Joe had carried neither gun nor light. But it was still a boldness that did not belong. . . .

The lion *was* different in some way, this animal he had appointed himself to find. And it was a long time before Jesse finally lost his questions and drifted off to sleep.

5.

Jesse opened his eyes to a morning that brooded in the wet and gray of a pelting rain. The sorrel waited nearby, head down and dismal, and the fire had died. He pushed deeper into that warm cocoon of wool and canvas, and debated the usefulness of going on.

For a moment, he dozed again, only to stir once more at the insistent rattle of rain across the canvas. There was no putting it off. Whether he went back to the house or continued to deceive himself about hunting a lion, he had to be up and doing.

It took more impulse than deliberation to finally make the move. Jesse crawled out and stood up, groaning at the soreness of his muscles. Moving stiffly, and still thick with sleep, he rolled up the bedding so that it would remain dry inside. With the rain spreading cold across the back of his shirt, he hurried to one of the bags and pulled out the heavy leather coat he had found in his father's closet. It was too small, not quite reaching his knees, but it was lined with lamb's wool and would keep him warm and dry. Too warm, probably; he had brought it along on the off-chance that the hunt would take him to the higher altitudes, where the bite of snow was still in the air.

There was no point in trying to build a fire. It would have taken too long to find enough dry wood as far as cooking was concerned. Jesse made do with a handful of dried apricots, and set about saddling the horse and getting everything in readiness to go.

Awake now, and having put all in order, the prospect of continuing upward seemed less unreasonable to him. He was no more optimistic than before. It was just a matter of deciding that, having come this far, he might as well go a little farther. The sorrel had a different idea, but Jesse gave him a gentle tug and aimed for the next ridge.

He made a slow zigzag of the climb. By that device, a wider swath of ground could be examined. And it was all that could be done in that weather. The higher they went, the more the clouds and rain closed about them. Visibility was reduced to perhaps fifty feet.

It was only frustrating, at first, to be blinded that way. A herd of elephants could have gone unnoticed, let alone a mountain lion. But after a while, it became in some way disturbing. He and the sorrel might as well have been cut off from the world and given one of their own— one filled with gray and shifting ghosts that moved just beyond the edges of recognition. Several times, Jesse found himself stopping and raising the rifle, knowing it was nothing—and yet not being very sure.

Perhaps it was that and nothing more—the brooding weight of a shadowed and dismal journey through a cloud. And certainly he had lived too long in a city to easily justify what he felt as being the sparkings of in-

stinct or intuition. But rain or otherwise, Jesse had the
uneasy sensation that he and the sorrel were being
watched and followed.

After a couple of hours, it was no longer enough
merely to glance over his shoulder and tell himself that
all his phantoms were made of raindrops. His nerve
ends insisted otherwise. He stopped then to listen and
watch, half expecting something to emerge from the
gloom behind them. Five slow minutes passed without
anything happening. But that prickly feeling persisted
and grew worse. Abruptly, Jesse turned the horse around
and cautiously began moving back along his own trail.

Perhaps it was foolish. He did not understand why it
seemed important to backtrack. It did not put an end
to blindness, and if they were being followed, a change
of direction was not going to make a difference.

But he stuck with his decision, and moving at a
quicker pace, it was not long before they had lost enough
altitude to reach the thinner edges of the clouds. Indeed,
after maybe an hour, a wind sprang up, and the world
they had lost gradually returned.

It was as if a slow suffocation had come to an end.
But with the lifting of clouds, and in a gentler, dying
rain, there was no sudden revelation; he and the horse
were quite alone. Jesse continued downward for a
while, studying the terrain for every conceivable kind of
cover it had to offer, and stopped only when, in the
immediate distance below, he caught sight of last night's
camp.

And still, nothing. Impatient and angry at having
wasted so much time and energy over what was obviously nothing more than his own nervousness, he de-

cided it was late enough to rest and break out some food. Letting the horse browse in the wet grass, Jesse found a rock to sit on and dejectedly ate a can of cold beef stew. When, he wondered, would he learn not to jump at shadows?

In a little while, he and the horse were on their way again, climbing. Not wanting to travel the same path a third time, he moved parallel to it at a distance of maybe fifty yards. And before they had gone a mile, the sun came out. The mountains and trees, cleaned by the rain, were suddenly very bright and beautiful. His spirits could not help being revived by the sight and feel of it. Putting the heavy coat back in the bag, he felt light and free, almost new, as if the day had begun with that moment and the gray morning had only been dreamed.

In very little time, they were almost as high as they had gone earlier. Yes, and right in the middle of that new and vibrant assertion of spring, Jesse made a discovery that cracked across his mind like a wire drawn taut: in the wet earth before him, the large, round print of a cat . . .

6.

It took Jesse a minute to regain his composure and do something more than stare. Moving on a few feet, he located a second print . . . and a third. There was a gap of several yards, then, and he had to cast around to find the trace again. A single impression, a cluster . . . sometimes it was only a small smearing of mud, or a patch of crushed grass. But it continued until he realized, with a chill, that the lion's path had crossed his own.

Jesse did not suppose that the warnings he had felt earlier were anything but false and coincidental, the workings of rain ghosts and shadows. But whether that was true or not, it was obvious now that the lion *had* been following him, and maybe still was, somewhere just out of sight.

The thought was uncomfortable, and he studied the trees around him. It did not matter that mountain lions were timid creatures, or that they had been known to follow man out of nothing more than harmless curiosity. Neither was there any question about it being just any lion, one of those chance encounters that could occur anywhere in the remaining wilds of the western ranges. Not until that erratic trace had included a clear print of the left forepaw did he remember that his father or Charlie, one of the two, had mentioned a missing toe. This was the same lion, and as had already been demonstrated, it was in some way different.

But whatever the nature of that particular lion, the situation had changed. He no longer had to move across those high slopes and ridges looking for mere hints of the animal's existence. Now he could hunt the lion itself. Not sure he entirely welcomed that fact, Jesse removed everything from the horse, including hackamore and saddle. With a slap on the rump, he sent the sorrel home.

Getting out his father's backpack, he loaded it with all the food he could comfortably carry. The remainder was left in the bags and hung from a high limb for safekeeping. Then, lashing bedroll, leather coat, and a coil of rope to the pack, he studied that place for a long time to mark it well in his mind.

Once again, Jesse wished he knew more about hunting and the nature of this particular lion. But no longer held to the limitations of a horse, and hoping it had been the right decision, he moved quickly and followed the tracks into late afternoon.

The tracks were never more than vague and tenuous things; they were hardly more than shadows, where shadows had no right to be. He lost them many times, and that he did not lose them permanently was probably a matter of coincidence—that of he and the lion both choosing the easiest line of travel. But there were occasions, in the final hours of the day, when it seemed that the lion was about to live up to its reputation for vanishing. As if his quarry had become vapor and no longer needed the earth, its trace simply stopped. The earth was drying, of course. And part of it had to be his own lack of experience; in each instance, after considerable delay, he *had* found them again. But there was still reason for wondering. In one case of regaining the lion's trail, Jesse had looked back and realized that there was a gap of maybe fifty yards . . . and the ground, for that space, was not different in any way that he could see.

Now, with the sun hanging on the western ridges behind him, Jesse had come to a region where soft earth gave way to stone. Here, the granite bones of the mountain broke the surface and thrust outward with barn-sized boulders and bluffs. Having a certain symmetry, vaguely stairlike, it reminded him of a flowerless Babylon. And here, too, the lion's traces once again faded out of existence.

Jesse stopped to rest and study the problem. Considering the direction the big cat had been traveling, up to this point, there seemed to be two possibilities: either the animal had continued toward the ridge by skirting along the edges of that place of stone, or it had gone straight to the nearest cleft between boulders, and from there to a ledge that angled upward and out of sight.

It depended, he supposed, on how the lion had come to see him: as a hunter, or as something that just happened to be moving along the same upward path. It was true that he had yet to fire the rifle. And if it was the lion that had approached his camp, last night, there had also been every indication that it was already gone by the time he sat up and started watching. In short, there had been no reason or chance, as yet, to betray his intentions with an openly hostile act. But not wanting to underestimate his adversary, Jesse decided it was safer to assume that the lion *did* know it was being hunted. And with that, he still did not have any answers . . . just questions. Was the cat trying to outdistance him, or was it taking cover and hiding?

"Might as well flip a coin!" he muttered under his breath.

But staring at that reddening expanse of stone, Jesse remembered yet another question that had bothered him earlier. The lion's den . . . what kind and where? Perhaps, he told himself, it was here.

He did not have to be reminded that, as one climbed toward timberline and the final reaches of the Sierras, such places as this became more and more frequent. It was only a thin possibility, then, that he had come to the lion's stronghold. But it broke the balance between two questions, and gave one the greater weight.

Shrugging into the backpack and getting up, Jesse went between the boulders and worked around that serpentine ledge until he reached the top of that first and lowest bluff. From there, it was necessary to jump a crevice and move back in the opposite direction along another ledge. Unlike the first, it narrowed down gradually to almost nothing. And having committed himself to it, he could not change his mind.

The ledge became small enough to be dangerous, and moving only slow inches at a time, Jesse became more and more alarmed. A fall here would either kill him outright or injure him so severely that he would not survive long enough to leave that place anyway. But just as the situation approached the impossible and threatened to strand him there, the ledge opened up to a shelf that was almost six feet square.

Gratefully, Jesse spent a few minutes to calm down, and then took the only way out. With nothing more than finger- and toeholds to work with, he climbed straight up for a dozen feet or so. And within two or three feet of the top, he failed—the face of the stone above him had turned smooth. In that failing light, he turned his head and studied the surface to the left, and it had what he was looking for; but he could not get to them without first going back down to the shelf and beginning again from a slightly different angle. And there was no time for that, now that the sun had gone down.

Jesse lowered himself a few feet to the most substantial holds he had encountered. There, knowing it was hardest to go down and needing badly to lighten himself, he carefully slipped out of the backpack. Lowering it with one hand, he caught the straps with his foot and lowered it farther still before letting it go. Hearing it land on the shelf, he eased himself downward—and could not find one of the toeholds. And slipping, he fell.

It happened too quickly to register in his mind. The next thing he knew, he had fallen across the backpack and was spreading his arms and legs to keep from rolling off the edge. Only when he stopped, and the world held still, did Jesse realize the significance of it. Then, nearly fainting with fright, he clutched himself to that shelf and trembled so hard that he could hear his teeth chattering.

When at last he could convince himself that he was not going to fall, and that he was indeed safe, twilight was deepening into the full dark of night. And there was no question that, if he was to remain safe, he had to stay there until morning. Jesse spread out the bedroll in that cramped space, and lacking both room and wood for a fire, had to content himself with eating a cold supper.

Knowing that it would soon be cold at that altitude, he removed only his boots and turned in. And feeling that hard stone beneath him, Jesse looked back at his coming there. He remembered the logic of it, but he also wondered if the lion had not deliberately led him into danger. There was no answer for it. But a cat . . . that particular lion . . . what kind of mind?

7.

Six thousand feet . . . seven . . . Jesse did not know how high he had gone. The house was far behind, and the great, vaulting backbone of the Sierra Nevada still towered above him. But from his ledge, the stars swarmed with a brilliance he had not known before. They appeared close enough, now, to envelop him in their frosty blaze, and he could not escape them to sleep.

Perhaps it was the absence of a fire. Deprived of its light, warmth, and familiarity, he felt lost and too small to still be a part of the world he had known. There was not even a wind, this night, to sound as a remembered voice and give him a last remaining thread. The connection seemed broken: This other world, this place of stone, could just as well have been another planet or an asteroid, free and wandering across the void. Sleep . . . he might have ended an unwanted voyage merely by closing his eyes and falling back to earth, but that seething, celestial silence persisted as a far and unheard shrieking in his ears.

And it might have been that he had drifted off for a time. It seemed to Jesse that he was seeing the stars *again.* Perhaps they were not where they were before. But if he had been asleep, why was he now awake? There was no doubt in his mind that he was too tired for the hardness of his bed to matter, and he had long since gotten over being uncomfortable about the height and smallness of the ledge. He watched and listened for a moment, wondering if something had happened.

It was pointless to puzzle over it. The best he could do was close his eyes again and try to relax. Very probably, he thought, he was just too tired to sleep soundly. But then a pebble fell, somewhere, sharply clattering . . . why? In his fatigue, Jesse had to search his mind, to make himself think about what might be living in those rocks. Some small nocturnal thing . . . mice? Or a lizard scuttling back into a crevice, now that stone no longer held the sun's warmth? Maybe, and he found nothing alarming about it; but before he could settle down again, another answer came in a quick and chilling way. Somewhere around him, the lion screamed.

Close at hand, and yet without direction in that baffling of rocks, it was a shattering thing that exploded across the senses, like the sound of a woman in mortal agony. Jesse scrambled out of bed, grabbed the carbine, and crouched there shaking and not knowing what to expect.

From that moment on, and though there was no moon for seeing, the night became alive with shadows. The very darkness *moved*—above him and to either side, and even out from the ledge in empty air, as if the lion knew no limits of earth and could be there as well . . . spirit . . . mist rather than flesh and bone. His senses were playing games with him; it had to be. But the

scream, the dry rattle of small rocks falling—these were
not imagined, and neither was the rasping, spitting
sound that shortly followed. The lion seemed closer.

On frightened impulse, Jesse pointed the rifle skyward.
The noise alone would drive that devil away. But then
he hesitated, and eased off the trigger. Shooting at nothing . . . that was what his father had taken to doing,
and it accomplished nothing. The whole idea of this
hunt was to reach the lion and kill it, not to start it
running again.

And yet, caught on that ledge until morning, what
could he do? It seemed to him that the initiative belonged to the lion, and it was not a comfortable thought.

The worst of it, perhaps, was being so nearly blind.
Jesse could see the sky, that higher rim of rock dimly out-
lined against the stars, and nothing more. And still unable to learn the direction of those furtive sounds, he
might as well have been deaf. In that situation, his only
choice was to settle down and wait, and try to think
his way through it.

There was no doubt that the lion was aware of his
presence, and indeed, knew exactly where he was. The
big question was why it had stopped and come back,
instead of making the most of that night for traveling.
Curiosity? Maybe, but the lion had already followed him
once, and then had gone on. Too, it was still possible
that the cat's den was there, somewhere, in that jumble
of granite. But if so, why had the cat come out of hiding?

Having yet to reach the next level above, Jesse had
no way of knowing what lay beyond it. And it occurred
to him that he might have unknowingly driven the lion
into a dead end . . . maybe he was blocking its way out.

It seemed unlikely, though, for something as lithe and agile as a cat. What was left, then, except the implication that, once again, the lion was not holding to the patterns of its own kind.

Jesse had to assume that the danger he felt was real and not imagined. And still he could do no more than what he was doing: crouching there with the rifle ready.

Shadows continued to swim in that dark air beyond the ledge, and he learned to ignore them after a while. And there were spaces of silence, but never for long—tiny sounds persisted around him, prickling along the edges of his nerves. He begged for the light of morning to come, but time was the inexorably slow turning of earth and stars.

After a time that held too much of eternity's empty cold, and still having reached no farther than the deepest part of the night, Jesse's ability to withstand that kind of punishment began to crumble. His every nerve end wanted to avoid the lion—it was too dark—and yet they fairly shrieked with impatience to have something happen and be done with it. And beneath this torment, his muscles had become cramped, and they ached with the need to stretch and move.

Knowing he could not make it through the rest of the night that way, Jesse wondered if he dared lie down for a little while. Arguing that it would not make any difference, as long as he kept his eyes open and stayed alert, he finally gave in to it. As if to make certain that it really was all right to relax, he took one more glance toward the stars—and suddenly saw what appeared to be the head of a lion looking down. His heart stopped and he felt the icy paralysis of terror, but somehow he raised the carbine and fired. Within that sharp explosion, Jesse heard the smaller sound of the bullet hitting something. In that same instant, the lion jerked back out of sight . . . and after the echoes died away, there was only silence.

Jesse stood up, shaking, convinced that the bullet had hit its mark. Not only had he heard the slug strike, it seemed to him that the lion had moved back faster than could be explained by mere reflex. He supposed he could have only wounded it—but, if so, why was it so quiet now? An injured animal would cry out, would it not? Cry out, or thrash about. Not liking the idea, Jesse clung to the fact of silence. Yes, the lion could be dead.

Jesse settled down for the night, knowing only a questioning, uneasy kind of peace. But there was no sleep. With the bedroll wrapped around his shoulders, he sat shivering and waited for morning.

8.

As if eternity could have an ending after all, those great, wheeling swarms of stars slowly faded until only the brightest of them remained. In that growing emptiness, when rumored morning was yet a faint and wisping gray, the sky and still-sleeping mountains fell into a different silence. And there was nothing in that time to warn Jesse, to tell him that his waiting was over. With his head resting on his knees, eyes closed, he was neither asleep nor awake, but drifting in what seemed an endless dark and cold. In his mind he saw a lion, and the lion appeared to be dead, and that was all he knew until the first birds noisily began to acknowledge a new day.

Exhausted and not wanting to move, Jesse lifted his head and stared bleakly at that emerging landscape. He wanted badly to have a fire and a cup of steaming coffee to drive the ice out of his bones. And above all, he wanted to find soft, warm earth somewhere and just sleep. But there was no time for that. Not yet.

Waiting until the light was better for climbing, Jesse once again made do with a handful of dried apricots. Then, rolling his bedding tight and putting the backpack in order—and wondering with sudden disgust why he

had not thought about the leather coat during the night
—he attached all of it to the rope, and tied the other end
to his belt. That way, with the climb made easier, he
could pull everything up after he reached the next level.

Ready now, and able to see the face of the rock clearly,
he began to climb. Remembering to bear more to the
left this time, Jesse carefully followed the cracks and
crevices for the grips they provided. And each time he
established himself in a position, he paused to work out
his next move in advance.

It was not a bad climb. The only difficulty he encountered was the growing pain and stiffness in his fingers; the granite still held the night's deep cold. But
little by little, he made it to the rim. Pulling himself over,
he sprawled on that welcomed horizontal space long
enough to catch his breath.

And when he could not hold curiosity off any longer,
Jesse sat up and looked around. . . . The expected carcass of a lion was not to be seen.

Stunned, refusing to believe his eyes, he got to his
feet intending to search the spaces behind some large
boulders to his left . . . surely the lion had crawled
there to die. But a tug at his belt reminded him of the
rope, and he had to stop to haul the backpack up.

Freeing himself of his gear, and leaving it there, Jesse
went to the boulders. Finding nothing, and still full of
disbelief, he moved away from them and along the foot
of another wall. It was not as straight up or as high as the
one he had just climbed, but a dying lion could not have
negotiated it. He thought then to go to the edge and
follow it around, knowing the lion could have fallen.
Finally reaching the place where he had climbed, and

even continuing past that point, he looked down at all the rocks and holes, the tangles of brush—and found not the slightest sign of the animal.

Going back to the general area above the ledge where he had slept, Jesse bent down and studied the flat surface of the granite itself. He had heard the bullet strike, and if it had only wounded the lion, then somewhere there had to be blood. One drop—he would have been satisfied to find just that one token of reality—something to refute all that was now beginning to crowd into his mind.

From that rim where he had seen the lion, all the way back to the next rising of stone, every square foot . . . *nothing*. And so the quarreling—his target had been so close at the moment of shooting that to have missed it would have been unlikely. But even allowing for the unlikely, the bullet had darted across that short space to make a sound of its own—not the hard sound of lead smashing into granite, but something softer than that, something yielding. Besides, from that angle, if the bullet had hit a stone surface, it probably would have ricocheted and gone singing off into the air. It was all very logical and reasonable, but the fact remained: no carcass, and no telltale trace of blood. There was nothing here to assure him, nothing to prove that his lion had been made of flesh and bone and not some kind of immortal smoke.

Maybe his father and Charlie Fergus had not been just frightened and superstitious; maybe the lion, if it could still be given the name, was other than natural and belonged to the dark, dead places of night, not to daylight and this vibrant world of a new spring.

Close to that panic that came when one's accepted

world began to totter and fall, Jesse coiled the rope and
shouldered his pack. Rather than go back the same peril-
ous way he had come, he made the next and easier climb,
and seeing a way out, traded granite for the softer earth
of the mountain.

He did not hesitate to point his steps downward; there
was nothing to reconsider. The creature had been too
much for him, and he wanted no more of its eerie games.
It was best to admit defeat and be done with it. And
why not? What could he or anyone do about a cat—a
thing that killed, left tracks, and yet remained out of
reach and as elusive as a moment of wind? Run out at
the barking of dogs, of course, and shoot just for the
sound it made. And then, having done no more than delay the inevitable, wait for another night when the devil
would come again. Quite clearly there was no alternative. . . .

No longer slowed by hunting and climbing, Jesse took
less than an hour to reach that place where he had left
the bag hanging in a tree. He had not thought to stop.
The supplies and that old saddle had to be left behind,
the expendables of an unfortunate and private little war.
But glancing in that direction, and then stepping closer,
he realized that the burlap was tattered and limp—
hardly more than a rag turning in the wind. In spite of
his supposed cleverness, some enterprising animal had
managed to reach the bag and rip it open. Only the
canned food had survived.

He supposed he had suspended it high enough off the
ground, without thinking about how close it was to the
limb. It was an ordinary mistake, and one that hardly
mattered now. He had more than enough food to get

back to the house. But it was also the final indignity. How could he have hoped to hunt a lion, to kill a shadow, when he could not even hold his own against the smaller and harmless creatures that lived in those mountains?

Jesse leaned against a tree, and closing his eyes, found himself close to weeping. Obviously, from this warning, it was time to stop. He needed a decent meal and, most of all, to get some sleep. Certainly there was no longer any necessity to push himself. The journey back to the house was all that remained, and it was pointless to hurry. He doubted very much that his father would have returned this soon. If he was going to return at all. . . .

Slipping against the rough bark, Jesse sat down and huddled against clamoring things. He was afraid, now; afraid to go back to the house. Eleven years . . .

It was hard to understand what, in innocence, people could do to each other. He knew that Jessica had never lost her love for Virgil. She simply could neither thrive in that rough world he made for her, nor ask him to give up what he had won from the mountains. And Virgil loved her enough to make no attempt to bring her back. Their marriage was neither a cage nor a prison, and that was as it should be. And yet, eleven years . . . a woman trying not to be lonely, and dying in San Francisco, and a man hanging on to a dream until it turned bitter.

Maybe if none of that had happened . . . if they had all stayed together and given that house the strength of a family . . . well, maybe he would not be where he was now, and Virgil would not be in a hospital, and maybe Jessica would be alive. And the lion might have been different. Maybe it would not have even existed.

Jesse could not explain the thought, especially in view of the fact that the cat had also terrorized the Ferguses and Joe. Nevertheless, in the breaking of a family, one pattern had been dropped and another set in motion. And he could not help feeling, as if destiny had somehow been altered, that the lion belonged to that second pattern and nowhere else. The thought was burdensome, and very probably the product of fatigue and failure. But whatever the truth, coincidence or something born in a man's solitude, the lion had brought his father to a final raging. And perhaps it had been fatal. Jesse did not know, and he was afraid to go back and find out.

And the house itself . . . it could not be seen from there. Only if he had gone higher, enough to dominate all the intervening ridges, would it have been visible again. But he saw the house in his mind: its roof and the barn's, two small squares swimming in a thin, blue haze. Now that he had exhausted the one alternative, having been defeated by the lion, he felt more certainly than ever that the house was slipping away and growing smaller, that even if he ran, it would be gone when he got there.

No. Jesse opened his eyes and looked at a landscape distorted by tears. The house was made of wood and glass and iron nails—of solid and tangible things. But what once was *home* . . . this part of the structure was caught in a shadow, and the darkness of it was deepening. He could not go home again, not and find it . . . and the darkness was a lion.

In a quickly growing rage, Jesse planted his boots hard against the earth and stood up. It was probably irrational or pointless, but if he could not go home, then he had to go the other way.

Opening the pack, he stuffed into it what he could of the remaining canned goods. All told, it looked like enough to last him a few days, but at that moment he did not really care. Wrestling the weight of it onto his back and grabbing the rifle, Jesse turned to begin climbing again.

When he reached the rocks again, a short time later, Jesse moved parallel to them and slowed down to a steadier pace. It would be new and unsearched ground from there on. Anger had not cured him of his fatigue, and he supposed it would be wise to stop and eat, and perhaps sleep for a while before going on. But he refused to give it a second thought. When the sun went down and he once again went into the long, cold night . . . that was the time for sleeping. Until then, he told himself, make the daylight count.

9.

It did not seem reasonable to question, now, what he had seen and fired at last night. That massive, almost triangular head was as vivid in memory as it was in the moment of seeing. The shape, its sudden motion, and the sound of the bullet striking . . . how, in an instant, could the mind manufacture so much that seemed so real? And yet, that it had been a trick of eye and frightened expectation was something that had to be considered . . . yes, and accepted, unless he wanted to surrender all good sense and, like the others, think of the lion as a ghost.

Well, Jesse told himself, maybe it is. But it hardly made a difference. Ghost, specter, wraith, demon, or simply a lion of unusual cunning, it had been destroying more than sheep, and it had to be hunted. And there was no doubt that he was woefully inadequate for the task, but he also knew of no decent alternative. More than sheep . . . a home, a remembrance already made fragile by time and miles, the death of his mother and the way a man had changed. . . .

Jesse did not hesitate in his climbing until he was on a level with the last and uppermost shelf of rock. There, he eased out of the pack and sat down to rest. It did not matter what the lion was, or what had or had not happened last night. He could not escape the idea that it originated here, that the creature's stronghold was somewhere in those masses of granite. The cat could be there now, in some deep recess, waiting quietly for the dark to come again. And perhaps not. How could he say that the lion, if it knew it was being hunted, had not led him away from its den? It might, in short, be foolish to waste time here while the devil moved farther and farther away; and it could be just as foolish to go on without first looking around.

After a few minutes of weighing one question against the other, Jesse realized that he did not really have a choice in the matter. One possibility existed here and now, and the other awaited him elsewhere, and so there was no reason not to approach them in that same order. But, more and more, he wondered if it was not almost a necessity to use dogs for hunting a lion. Without them, it was apparently a matter of luck. And luck was such an elusive companion.

Taking only the carbine, he returned to the rocks and stepped out on a huge slab that dominated the whole slope. From that vantage point, he saw that the outcropping was perhaps one hundred feet wide and maybe three times again as long. He could not quite see that part of it where he had looked for the lion's carcass.

It was not a discouraging prospect. The worst of it, as far as climbing was concerned, was down below, where he had spent the night. Jesse saw no need for going over that part of it again. And a large portion of that chaotic slope was composed of massive monoliths, which would both reduce and simplify his search; they occupied sizable areas with solid and inhospitable stone. Too, where there were spaces, hollows, and clefts between the giants, most were open to the sky and therefore useless. For all its stony confusion, then, it offered fewer chances for a lion's den than he had expected. Indeed, he wondered if he had not been mistaken in suspecting that place at all. But, whatever the case, it probably would not take more than an hour to find out.

But Jesse still did not rush to begin the search. Instead, he sat down and tried to think like a lion. Or a ghost. He grimaced at the uncertainty he had come to feel, and closed his eyes. If he had seen the lion last night, and not just something conjured out of fright and shadows, then its presence might have had some bearing on the whereabouts of its lair. Presumably, the lion saw him as a threat. And if that threat were quite close at hand, was the animal likely to come from hiding to seek the danger out? Jesse did not think so. He could understand the lion wanting to know exactly where he was and what he was doing, but not at the possible expense of betraying its hiding place. It seemed to him that the lion would not make such a move unless—*unless*, he thought and opened his eyes—the danger was still a fair distance away. In short, if his reasoning was valid and *if* there was a den here, it almost had to be somewhere in the higher rocks . . . maybe only a matter of yards from where he was sitting.

Feeling uneasy at the thought, Jesse threw the carbine's lever to open the breech and eject the shell casing from last night's wasted shot. It made only a tiny clatter-

ing as it bounced across granite, but the sound was somehow startling. He hesitated for a moment and then
worked the lever again, slowly, watching the next cartridge slide into the chamber. Remembering to lower the
hammer into the safety position, he stood up and quietly
made his way down through an arch of leaning boulders
to the next level.

The rocks there were not entirely barren. Perhaps because that place was close to the top, and knew a small
amount of runoff from the mountain when the rains
came, its seams and depressions had patiently collected
a meager treasure of soil. It was just enough to support a
little grass and a few gnarled, twisted pines which,
though no more than a few feet tall, looked as if they
could have been thousands of years old.

Jesse had hopes, at first, that this presence of soil
would also hold the possibility of tracks, some small
trace to confirm that his thinking had been good, and
that the lion was here somewhere. But he was soon disappointed; maybe those deposits of earth were too small
and random to match an animal's more deliberate lines
of travel.

Returning his attention to the rocks and wandering
among them, he did find holes and recesses, and faint
indications that they were being used: scratch marks,
droppings, a bit of hair moving in the wind. But they
were smaller animals. Fox, skunk, bobcat, porcupine, a
large variety of rat . . . he did not know enough about
animals to read the signs, and so could not identify
them.

There was one place, beneath an overhanging boulder,
that was big enough to accommodate a lion. Not know-

ing how else to go about it, Jesse got down on his knees
and, rifle ready, moved into it very slowly. But it quickly
proved to be too shallow and too open to the world to
satisfy what, he assumed, would be a cat's need for
secrecy.

Both relieved and disappointed, he crawled out and
sat on his heels for a moment, questioning the worth of
what he had just done. Those other holes . . . he wondered if the homes of smaller creatures ruled out the
proximity of a lion's den. And again, it was something
for which he had no answer.

Having exhausted that level's possibilities, he looked
for a way down to the next. It seemed, after a few
minutes, that he might have to climb back to the top
and leave the rocks, and then return from a lower point.
But he finally found a steeply pitched pathway, if it
could be called that, snaking down between two high
walls of granite that were no more than ten or twelve
inches apart.

It required that he enter sideways with his chin
jammed into his right shoulder. Because of the rifle,
Jesse had only one arm to brace himself against the
steepness. And that arm also kept him from seeing; each
step, on that loose and rocky surface, was blind. He very
quickly regretted his choice. But, committed to that
pinching space, there was no changing position or turning back.

Several times he nearly fell. It cost him skin on his
arm, and he felt a raw, burning place on the side of his
face. Tense, and growing angrier by the minute, he finally stopped and pressed his face against cool granite.
In that place and at that moment, it was easy to wonder

at this spectacle of himself: exhaustion, fear, exposure to
the elements, hunger, the risking of death or injury, all
because of one stupid animal—a lion that, in some way,
had to be different! Jesse blinked the sweat out of his
eyes. No, not stupid, but cunning. If there was any stu-
pidity involved, it was probably in his own knack for
blundering into the wrong places and making the hunt
more difficult than it had to be.

It took another ten minutes to negotiate the remainder
of that precipitous passage. In sudden freedom, and
conscious of the time lost, Jesse quickly resumed his
search for the lion's den.

Unlike the area above it, this segment of the outcropping was small and filled almost entirely by vertical
thrustings of stone. There were few places to walk, and
few directions to take. In less than a dozen minutes, he
explored three quarters of it without finding shelter for
anything more than lizards or mice. Because it had such
a jumbled sameness, and because he was already watching for a way down to the next section of rocks, Jesse
looked twice before he really saw the recess—the patch
of darkening shadow that led deep into stone.

He stopped and took a step back, and stood there to
let it settle in his mind. The opening was large enough,
and from what he could see, it seemed like it might be
deep enough. Keeping eyes and ears tuned for any signs
of life, Jesse slowly approached the entrance and dropped
to his knees. From there, he could see more than six
feet before the darkness took over. And the floor of the
entrance was covered with a layer of dust that had been
disturbed. He stared at it, trying to find even part of a
recognizable print. But either a wind had sent that dry,

fine dust to drifting around, or the hole's occupant had created too much of a disturbance in entering or leaving. The traces were too vague and muddled to read.

Not knowing what kind of animal lived there, Jesse was left with two alternatives. He could hide among the rocks and wait for it to come or leave—assuming, of course, that it had not or would not catch his scent and remain out of sight. Or he could enter the hole, and perhaps find the answer quickly.

The second alternative was not at all pleasant to consider. But again, if the lion did not have a den in those rocks, the sooner he found out and got going, the better chance he would have of overtaking the lion elsewhere. He simply could not take a chance on spending maybe the rest of the day there and discovering that the hole belonged to a bear or coyote. And besides, although it was not wise to enter an animal's lair, Jesse had a feeling that a good, fiery torch would discourage an attack.

He stood up, and remembering that the northern side of that level afforded an easy way down to earth, grass, and trees, he went to gather the makings for a torch. He had never made one before, but the idea seemed simple enough.

Jesse gathered slender lengths of dead pine and tied them in a bundle, with twistings of dry grass stuffed into the upper half. Satisfied that it would catch easily and burn for the few minutes he needed, he also thought to pull one branch out at the bottom end to serve as a handle. Gripping it and the rifle barrel in his left hand, he found that he could hold and aim the carbine with very little difficulty.

When he reached the hole again, Jesse pulled the

hammer back so that the rifle would be ready to shoot, and then struck a match to light the torch. The grass caught first, and then the pine, and it began to burn as he had hoped it would. Quickly taking advantage of its bright and noisy flame, Jesse left the friendly sky behind.

It was fairly easy going for the first six or eight feet. Then the passage narrowed down and made an abrupt turn to the right. A few steps found him under a lowering ceiling, and crouching now, he came to a stop. Ahead of him, perhaps a dozen feet away, he saw the rocks opening up to what seemed to be a small room.

There was little doubt that he had come to the den itself, and confronted so closely by the possibility of it belonging to the lion, Jesse anxiously tried to appraise his own position. His first realization was that it would no longer be as easy to handle both torch and rifle in that confining space. He supposed he could put the torch down and use both hands for the carbine. But then there would not be as much light for a target, and the torch might not even last long enough lying on its side. And given those circumstances, he also realized that there was too much risk of only wounding the animal; if that happened, he probably would not have time for a second shot, and that cramped passage offered no protection against the fury that would come exploding out of the dark.

He was frightened by what he had come to, and for that moment could not think or move. All he could do was crouch there, watching with constantly startled eyes the shadows leaping from flame to make the dim room before him so alive with threatening shapes.

Only when an ember fell and burned his hand did

Jesse snap out of it and, though still afraid, start using his head again. Those shadows did not cease to be menacing, but it occurred to him that he was not hearing anything beyond the crackling of the torch . . . surely if one of those shapes was the lion or another animal getting ready to charge, it would be growling or spitting at him. And unless he went too close, it was not likely to jump him while he was brandishing a torch; he remembered coming to that conclusion outside.

And so, having collected himself to that extent, the rest became obvious. He would shoot if attacked, but his real purpose was to identify the den's occupant. If it was there, and if it was the lion, then he would make a cautious retreat and wait for it outside—maybe even devise a way to smoke it out.

Calmer now, Jesse took a few steps closer to the den. The shadows grew thin and dispersed, and his approach did not earn a warning response. Indeed, when he dared the last remaining feet, he found the room to be empty. And if there had been an animal inside when he entered the hole, there was no reason for it to still be around; leading on from that room was another and smaller passage, and at its end, the diffused glow of daylight.

The torch was now burning low and too close to his hand. Running out of time, he quickly bent down and examined the dusty hollows of the floor. Jesse could not see well enough to look for prints, but he found tufts of hair. Grabbing a sample, he turned and hurried outside.

Back in the light of day, he studied the hair, and it seemed too long for a lion. But it was also a dark, reddish brown, and that was what decided it for him. The den did not belong to the lion, but was apparently the wintering place of a bear.

Reluctantly starting down to the next level, Jesse took one look and realized that he had finally come to the place where he had expected, earlier, to find the lion's dead body. He was finished with those rocks, then. It was time to leave and go on.

Jesse was disappointed, putting that place of granite behind and climbing back to where he had left his pack. There was no telling whether the lion had waited somewhere nearby to watch him with a continuing curiosity, or if it had used the time to hurry into the distance.

But very clearly it had abandoned that place and pointed its steps upward. There in the soft earth, only a few yards from that top layer of granite where he had begun the search, Jesse found a pawprint with the telltale missing toe. Letting his breath out at the irony of having come that close before, and not seeing it, Jesse cradled the carbine in his arm and quietly began to follow.

10.

It could be wondered why, at last, the lion chose to go so high. . . .

That it was happening was not a part of his awareness, at first; there was no real suggestion or warning of it, no sudden difference to reveal the lion's intention and set it apart from all that had happened before. At the moment he abandoned the rocks, Jesse had learned that the lion was still climbing, and its vague traces continued to lead him upward for the rest of that day and into sundown. The big cat was still somewhere in the silent distance above him when he was forced to stop and make camp for the night.

And that was the way it had always been. . . .

Back at his father's house, when that troubled man first spoke of a demon and called it a lion, it was a creature that came down at night from somewhere higher in the mountains. And so how else could it be considered except as being a part of the mountains and the night? It belonged there no less than did the rocks and trees, and the bright swinging of the moon. To even think of the lion was also to look *upward*.

There was only one thing, one hint to speak of differ-

ence and give it measure; and at that, the possibility was
still merely implied. It was not apparent in those accustomed tracks. And neither did it come in any way from
the lion itself; its mind was no more readable than the
wind. Time should have told him the significance of an
unceasing direction, but time also buried meanings in its
own growing monotony. Instead, it was the night itself
that whispered of what was taking place. The darkness
held a deeper cold than before . . . the air smelled of
winter's ice. And hear the stars? Almost. They were closer
and more incredible than ever.

So high . . . and *why?*

As lightly as an echo, the possible significance of it
brushed across his thoughts, and then was gone. Jesse
was too exhausted from the constant climbing, too full of
food, and too lulled by a comforting fire. As if hearing
a far voice somewhere in that wilderness, he lifted his
head questioningly for a moment, and then surrendered
to sleep.

Maybe it was a lessening of haze and the growing
number of open spaces, and maybe he had been too preoccupied with the tracks and watching for the lion. But
after climbing halfway through that next day, and stopping to rest for a time, Jesse suddenly became aware of
how clearly the final ridges and high towers of the Sierras rose before him. It was with this startling confirma-
tion of how far they had traveled that he began to wonder, finally, what the lion had in mind.

Strictly from the standpoint of being pursued, the direction made no sense; not when an easier line of escape
existed in all other directions. By turning away to the

north or south, or by even dropping back to the west
again, the lion doubtlessly could have outdistanced its
tormentor. The hunt would have very quickly become
pointless.

But never mind what seemed logical and what did not,
the tracks revealed not the slightest evidence of hurrying,
and led unswervingly toward that higher world where
the air was thin and much of earth and life still waited,
sleeping under winter's snow.

Why? In choosing the more difficult path, perhaps it
planned to destroy him . . . it had to be wondered. But
whatever the answer, a remembered valley and its season of spring were being left far behind. . . .

11.

There beneath jagged, cloud-thrusting peaks, where bitter wind struck the harps of earth and made a great and frightening music, the lion's tracks were the only reality; a reality that was dubious and fragile at best. At times, they were strong black punctures in crusted snow, or shapeless smears in the ooze of newly exposed earth. And sometimes they went fading across stone where, in winter winds, snow had not been able to cling. There were spells when the prints seemed quite old, a lingering reminder of a creature that had walked across the mountain on a now distant day . . . and then they would appear to be so fresh that they might have been made just minutes before.

But not once was there a glimpse of the lion itself . . . neither a tiny sparking of motion nor furtive image anywhere in that massive push of earth to tell him that it was near or far, real or unreal.

Ghost, shadow . . . during the long, hard climb, Jesse had come more and more to suspect that what he fired at, the other night, had been nothing other than a creation of his own imagination. And now, in this high place, his underlying trust that the lion was flesh and blood—

his whole, unvoiced quarrel with his father and Charlie
—was once again beginning to totter and crumble. The
stands of pine were still fairly dense, that close to the
timberline. There were, however, quite a few more barren spaces, white expanses of windswept alpine meadow
that the lion had to cross . . . and the tracks said that it
did. *How*, without being seen?

It could be argued, of course, that the lion was farther
ahead than he thought; a few days had not made him an
expert in judging the age of the tracks. But neither could
Jesse ignore those frequent intervals in which he could
also see for considerable distances into the country
ahead. And so it still did not seem reasonable. . . .

The lion's trail had finally swung north, somewhere
near the ten-thousand-foot level, and no longer forced
him to do much climbing. But the air was thin, and
unaccustomed to it, Jesse was constantly tired and not
entirely clear of mind. It was hard enough just to move,
and remain alert, without also being nagged by questions he had already asked a hundred times over. But
had an irrational mind created a demon, or had a demon
made a man irrational? The Ferguses and Joe gave the
support of added numbers to his father's belief; but was
that because the lion *was* some kind of supernatural creature, or because Virgil Seward's frightened ravings were
contagious?

There were tangible things to hang on to and remember, things that should have helped keep his own mind
straight in the matter. The tracks were not an illusion,
and neither were the dead sheep or the screams that had
scraped across his nerves. And a man had been mauled.
And yet, in the absence of seeing what he pursued, there

were times when he wondered if he was not following
the embodiment of all that had torn at his father in the
last eleven years . . . the bitterness of losing wife and
son, loneliness and the growing weight of isolation, and
trying to keep that place going even though it had been
a dream for more than just himself. It was as if this essence of his father had been loosed on the mountains in
the vain hope that it would evaporate under the sun—as
if this were his quarry, and not flesh born of lions.

Jesse faltered and stopped to scoop up snow in his
hands. He scrubbed his face with it and breathed deeply,
for a few minutes, to clear his mind. The essence of a
man. He wished he could go down again, back where he
belonged.

Late that afternoon, the tracks led Jesse to the fresh
carcass of a deer. He could not imagine why it had gone
this high so soon, abandoning new spring grass to wander back into winter. But the doe obviously had been
sick and starved when it came to the end. And at first, it
was his assumption that the deer had fallen there after
the lion had passed. Except for a few old scars, there
was not a mark on that bony and wasted body. But then,
paying more attention to the snow around the deer, he
realized that it had been disturbed by more than the
doe's falling.

Dropping to his knees, Jesse searched that delicate
neck with his fingers. It still held a hint of warmth . . .
and it was *broken.*

Feeling a prickling sensation along his spine, Jesse
looked quickly around him, and watched the country
ahead. Maybe the lion had killed it for the sake of killing,

or maybe the deer had crossed its path by accident and the lion had lashed out with nervous anger . . . but Jesse knew that it could also mean that he had interrupted the cat before it could feed. And this, of course, would mean that the lion was not very far away. Perhaps the hunt was close to being over.

With the kind of energy that comes of growing optimism, Jesse hurried along the tracks for another hour. But he did not see the lion. Neither was there any sound to betray it; the wind was too loud in his ears. But if there was a reason for hope, it was soon lost to a darkening sky, a strengthening of that wind, and the first stinging particles of falling snow.

The best he could do was quickly seek out the shelter of trees and rocks. There, he made a lean-to from the canvas part of his bedroll, and gathered what dry wood he could in the little time that remained. It was a whipped and sorry thing, but he somehow got a fire going. There was even a chance to wolf down a half-cooked meal before retreating into his blankets.

And that was all that could be done. Again, Jesse wished he could have gone down—back to the gentle, spring evening that waited somewhere below the storm. But he had to sit it out; there were no alternatives.

By nightfall, the intensity of the storm had reached such proportions that there was no doubt in his mind as to what had come to strike at those mountains. Spring? What the calendar said hardly mattered. It was a blizzard.

12.

The world could have been dying, for all he knew. What he felt and heard were beyond his comprehension. That wind—there were no words for it; violent gusts grew in blackness, and became something more than violence. With the roaring of some great, cosmic entity, it deafened the mind. Snow no longer fell but hurtled sideways, and the night was filled with the awful artillery of breaking trees. And the very mountains themselves seemed to tremble.

Sleep was totally out of the question, of course. Behind tortured and snapping canvas, Jesse could do no more than huddle in his blankets and fight to keep an almost useless fire going. The wind stole most of its heat, and sent its smaller embers scattering out into the dark. The heavy coat probably made the slight difference between being cold and freezing. But there was no courage to be found in the fact that, for *that* moment, he was holding his own. Never before had he felt so lost and so thoroughly alone. The night was completely without alternatives. He could not run from it or cry for help, and if anyone had known of his whereabouts, he still would have been beyond reaching. He was indeed, for all that could be done, the last person on earth.

And one of the worst things about the storm was not knowing what to expect of it. Blizzards had always happened elsewhere—they had been something to read about, or to see in a television newscast—something remote, and in that sense, meaningless. If they had occurred during those eight years in his father's house, then he did not remember them . . . perhaps because, in a snug house, storms mattered little, and a small child would not have been permitted to go outside. But how long would it last? How long could the storm sustain that much force? Just a few hours more . . . a day or two . . . maybe a week? He did not know, and what he heard sounded like forever.

And the lion . . . there was no doubt in his mind that the hunt was over. Even if blizzard's end found him with enough food and able to travel, it would be useless to continue. The lion, like himself, must have been forced to take cover and for that reason probably would not be very far away. But where? All that snow and wind would have quickly obliterated the last traces of its existence.

There was nothing left, then, except to sit it out if he could, and then try to go down. Down to where snow would have turned to rain, and on down from there to the house, knowing very well that, sooner or later, the lion would come again to raid.

Somewhere at a time when it should have been close, Jesse anxiously began watching for the dawn. But it never came; not in that black and howling wind. It must have been at least eight or nine o'clock before a hidden sun rose high enough, above the mountains, to reach the western expanses of the storm and give it a pale, uncertain light. And then it hardly seemed to matter. What was there, finally, to see? He could make out rocks and the tortured trees closest to him, and that was all. Beyond those shadows, nothing. An unfathomable and constant explosion of white.

The wind rose and fell and was anything but constant. But there were times now when the quieter intervals seemed to last longer. And yet he could not be sure it was not just himself. How long could one exist at the heart of violence before becoming numbed or a little deafened to it? Such things were difficult to measure when it was hard to remember the quality of silence and peace. But even if the storm's force was diminishing, the difference was too little to have meaning . . . not now, anyway. If it was the first hint that, somewhere in time, the storm had an ending, then that ending was too far away. Jesse could not remain where he was and wait it out; his supply of firewood was gone.

In preparing for the night, he had pretty well exhausted the nearby sources of fallen wood. What remained was either too small or too big, or too old and crumbling into wormy dust. There were other stands of trees, of course, somewhere out in that white. But it would take too many trips, and he was not at all sure he could find his way back . . . and since he would have to leave his rifle and the pack in order to carry the needed amount of wood, there was too much risk of being separated from them.

Searching for some alternative to that dying fire, Jesse vaguely remembered something about burrowing into snow and using it as an insulating cover. Dogs did it, and people had done it . . . he was certain of that much, but could not recall the conditions that permitted it. But as the heat of the fire failed, and more of that bitter cold closed in around him, he lost any stomach he might have had for trying such a thing.

Having no other answer to the situation, Jesse rolled up the canvas and blankets and put his pack in order. He stood there for a moment, reluctant to leave the fire. Its death, though, was only minutes away, and so he finally walked off into that icy blast.

The difference was both brutal and extreme. Away from the comparative shelter of trees and rocks, the wind became something he had not known before. It sucked the breath from his mouth and all but blinded him. There was no standing upright against it. And the flying snow, so long thought of as soft and fluffy flakes, struck him as would a swarm of hard, stinging insects. The one blessing of the wind was that, in those open spaces, the accumulation of snow was not yet enough to cause trouble. Reduced to a fine powder, it smoked across the ground in swift currents and did not stop until there was a tree, a rock, or a fallen limb to catch it. But it would not stay that way, not if the storm lasted. Those few inches were a warning.

His intention, of course, was to go down. The storm belonged to those high places where winter was slower to end its reign and leave. It stood to reason that if he could make it down for three or four thousand feet, he would be out of the snow and wind—or at least the worst of it. And yet it was hard to imagine that somewhere below him and not so very far away, there was a different climate, a different season . . . a gentler world. He could not entirely remember what it was like to be warm, and rested, or well fed, or how it was to squint into bright and golden sunlight. But that better place *was* there, and he had to believe that it was and go down . . . and he did not know how. Where? Which way was down?

There was no such thing as direction. Jesse could not find the slightest hint of the sun's location. Visibility was limited to a few yards, and in the more open areas, he too frequently experienced the phenomenon known as white-out: a condition in which there was no longer any dividing contrast between ground, horizon, and sky. When it happened, he knew only an absolutely blank, featureless white wherein only the sensations of wind and gravity remained. Deprived of anything visible to relate to, he suffered vertigo and often had to sit down and wait for the white-out to pass.

But perhaps worst of all were those times when Jesse did find himself going down, when, letting himself be encouraged, he hurried to make the most of it, and sooner or later found the slope bending upward again.

And so, no matter what he wanted or tried, what could he do but wander helplessly and with dwindling hope . . . blind, exhausted, half frozen, and totally at the mercy of the blizzard?

It went that way for hours, his walking in that deepening snow serving no purpose other than that of maintaining a minimum of bodily warmth. If he stopped, then most certainly he would collapse and die; and as if waiting for this to happen, there were shadows following, circling in the white, and sounds beneath the greater voice of the wind—minor choruses of screaming. Lion, demon, tortured trees, or his own protesting soul . . . Jesse did not know what was real and what was dream. And as that day wore on, without any sign of difference, there were intervals when he ceased to care and would have stopped and let himself go to sleep, and die, had he known how to end the habit of struggle.

It came like its own kind of ghost—dim shape, a different kind of darkness emerging from white—a shadow that somehow stood still. Jesse stopped and swayed for a long time, looking at it and not knowing what it was. The wind had to gust and clear the air for an instant before, in the numbness of his mind, he realized that the geometry of it was man's, that he had reached shelter. A small cabin, dark with age and splintered by time, its door banging in the wind.

13.

Stumbling the last few steps, Jesse hurried into the cabin. Finding that the door could be locked with a massive, hand-wrought hook and eye, he closed it against the wind, and in that sudden peace, turned to what good fortune had provided.

There was just one small window, which was boarded over, and so the only light he had was the little that filtered in, here and there, through chinks between the logs. Lighting a match, he made a quick survey of the space and made certain that, in closing the door, he had not trapped a skunk or any other fugitive from the storm that might prove to be troublesome company. But he also wanted to know where to spread his bedroll, and to see if there was a place to build a fire, and indeed, if there was anything to burn. Too, some kind of light would be useful . . . a kerosene lamp, maybe, or at least something better than matches and that would burn long enough for him to get settled in.

Jesse had to move closer to the center of the floor and strike a second match before he became aware that the floor was simply packed earth, and that there was a fireplace at the opposite end of the room—and to the right of it, a small, cluttered shelf. Making it to the shelf before the match went out, he lit another and found a collection of rusted cans, a box of handmade nails, a broken-handled hatchet, a box of salt . . . and a whiskey bottle with three inches of candle stuck in the top.

Almost grinning with his good luck, he touched the match to the wick. In its soft glow he put his pack down and spread the bedroll out on the floor. The fireplace proved useless, having fallen in on itself. But he supposed he could not expect everything.

Not knowing whether he wanted to eat first or just sleep, Jesse sat on his bedding and merely stared at that place for a while.

The cabin could have been a relic of the Gold Rush, surviving still in the dry air of that high altitude. Such a thing was not at all uncommon. And then, too, it might have belonged to more recent times. The quest had diminished but not ended with the dying of the rush; men still wandered the Sierras, dreaming the fevered dream of finding another Mother Lode. But whatever its history, the cabin was little more than a shell now, and for a long time had been shelter to nothing more than mice. Their droppings were everywhere. And thinking of the mice, he supposed the candle's survival was something of a miracle . . . only the tall, smooth sides of the bottle had prevented them from reaching it.

In his slower appraisal of the room, Jesse found two other items left by its last human inhabitant: a cracked and yellowing fragment of mirror, which rested on nails driven into the logs, and a pair of snowshoes hanging from a rafter.

Jesse guessed that their owner, which for some reason

he imagined to have been an old man, had left this place
in summer. Possibly knowing that he would not be coming back, he had left the shoes on the chance that somebody would need them. There was a custom in wilderness areas, he had heard, in which shelters were left
open and stocked with some of the necessities for survival.

The snowshoes would have to be repaired somehow;
the years had not been kind. Their frames were splitting,
and some of the webbing was broken. But it was still
tempting to think in terms of divine providence or a
remarkable quirk of fate. No matter how long the storm
lasted, or how deeply it buried that high world, he could
walk out.

Jesse closed his eyes for a moment, and drifted . . .
and jerked them open again. It was catching up with
him now, all the missing sleep, the climbing, fighting
the cold, and what had been the strain of knowing he
had little chance of surviving the blizzard.

Forgetting the notion of eating, he stood up to get the
candle; there was no point in letting it burn for nothing,
and he had already used an inch of it. Taking it off the
shelf and thinking he would keep it by the bedroll, he
passed near the mirror, and the reflection of the candle
caught his eye.

He had not thought to look, but went closer and saw
himself—someone—reddened eyes with a kind of fever in
them, dark circles . . . skin burned by weather, and the
wide crust of a scab from temple to cheek . . . dirt, and
the stubble of beard: All of it combined to create a
stranger. Especially the eyes—they might have belonged
to a madman, a wretched soul who, in the pursuit of

devils, had become some kind of devil himself. Where was the young man whose mother was still alive, and who had yet to know of a lion?

Suddenly frightened by it, Jesse pushed away from the image. He quickly turned and sat down in the center of his bedding . . . sat there, trembling, and stared at the candle. The stranger in the mirror—he was not so sure that the face had not been Virgil's.

"Stop it!" He yelled, and startled by the sound of his own voice, forced his attention back to the needs of the moment. His boots . . . they would, he decided, be all that he removed. The cabin kept the snow and that killing wind away, but it was drafty and just as cold as it was outside. Crawling into bed, Jesse supposed that, between the heavy coat and the layers of blankets and canvas, he would be reasonably warm.

Blowing the candle out and burying himself, he listened to the storm raging outside and wondered how long he would have to stay there. But for now, at least, he was all right.

As Jesse fell quickly toward sleep, the now accustomed howling of the wind was first to fade from awareness. Only the rattling of the door remained—and then it, too, was lost.

14.

Sleep was a deep and tortured thing somewhere below and far away from now, in a time of its own. Time or times . . . there was no order to what came to him. Jesse saw the sheep dying again, and then with a flickering of whatever light it was that made a dream, it was San Francisco—and the sheep were lying in the middle of Stanyan Street, drawing a crowd. His mother hurried to him from across the street and led him away from there. Jessica might have been crying, and she kept saying it was time to go home. But they never got there . . . she was gone, and he stood alone in Union Square watching the pigeons flying, and wondering why they would not come down.

He had only wanted to feed them. . . .

Jesse rose up on his elbows and saw that the thin lines of light, which had come between the logs before, were gone. The long night had come somewhere in his sleep, and he did not know how far it was to morning. Outside, the wind still howled with a maniacal raging; those old timbers were strong and only trembled in the onslaught.

But the door rattled, as if the wind knew its weakness and was trying to come in.

He thought of lighting the candle and eating something now. Food, he knew, would lessen the effects of thin air, that bitter cold, and the exhaustion that still weighed him down. But somewhere in the middle of reaching for a match, those same elements pushed him back into sleep.

Jesse did not know how much longer he slept, or how long he remained in the half world that followed—a place where he was neither asleep nor awake but possessed by a kind of dreaming, and by realities that seemed like dreams. Maybe it was, in part, the wind; its constant presence was almost hypnotic. But unable to climb out of it, he wandered along that vague division between slumber and delirium.

The night went its full cycle in that manner, and at least part of another day passed: Light again came to filter through spaces between the logs. And toward the end of whatever time was passing, a dream came to him . . . or a moment of reality. With half-closed and staring eyes, he was watching his boots—the snow caked on them had yet to melt and still looked fresh, as if he had only just arrived—and then he heard a scratching at the door . . . claws . . . and a screaming that joined the wind and was full of madness.

Something had come to him . . . the *lion* . . . he could almost see it out there . . . something made of smoke and fire and immortal shadows. It knew he was inside and wanted in, its claws pulling curls of wood from the door.

In reality, or in a dream, Jesse crawled out of his bed-roll, got the carbine, and cocked it. There was no avoiding that moment—as if having been summoned to some final point of inevitability, he went to the door with every intention of opening it to that satanic creature. No matter the outcome, the nightmare had to be ended.

But while he very clearly remembered reaching for the hook, and feeling the biting cold of its metal, and even beginning to lift it from its eye, there was nothing after that. Dream or reality, it simply stopped there and was without a conclusion. He knew nothing more, just a sudden slipping into something deep, a blackness and an unexpected peace.

15.

It was, perhaps, the silence that awakened him. Jesse did not move for a long time, but waited deep in his blankets, trying to convince himself that it was, indeed, silence rather than an illusion or some kind of deafness of the mind. But the quiet was real, and neither was it just for the moment; no new rising of the wind came to destroy it.

Sticking his head out and watching the darkness of the cabin, he saw that it was daytime. Pale light came through the cracks in the walls . . . pale enough to signify the beginning of day, or its final hour. But there was no direction to it, no favoring of one side of the cabin over the other, and Jesse realized that the quality of light indicated not the time but the continuing presence of clouds overhead.

The time of day hardly mattered to him. Or so it seemed, at first. He was too relieved, too happily bewildered by the fact that the blizzard was over and gone and that he had survived it. Only when he crawled out of the bedroll, and once again felt the sharp bite of cold, did he think of the snow and the wisdom of using the light to travel as far as possible, downward. And because of his feeling of having been there for a long time, and having slept for what seemed an age, Jesse made the assumption that it was afternoon. He had to hurry, then.

Rested, but shaking from hunger, he knew he had to eat before he did anything else. And now that he was preparing to leave the cabin, he dared consider building a fire there on the floor. Smoke would be a problem, probably, and there was not much in the cabin that he could use for fuel. The object now, however, was not to heat the cabin but to warm some food.

Jesse gathered a pile of twigs brought in by rats and wind over the years. It was dry and would serve as kindling. Using the broken hatchet he had found on the shelf, he ripped the boards from the window and split them. It was not much, and would burn quickly. But all he asked of it was to heat some beans and a can of meat. His hands shaking, he touched a match to it.

With the window open, the smoke was not something that could not be endured. The warmth from the fire was a luxury, and the food smelled fabulous; and even though it came from a cloudy day, the added light from the window lifted his spirits to where he was almost cheerful.

He had been without food, and in the cold, and breathing that thin air too long; he felt, after eating, a deep lassitude. Sitting before the last of the fire, Jesse could barely keep his eyes open. The temptation to crawl back into the bedroll was strong. But rather than give in to it, he stood up and got the snowshoes down. The next order of business, before leaving, was to see what could be done to repair them.

Considering the materials on hand, there was only one answer. He had to rip narrow strips of canvas from his bedroll cover and, squeezing the splits shut, wrap the frames as tightly as he could. And where the rawhide webbing was broken, the most he could do was tie in new lengths of leather with what could be spared from his bootlaces. It was a sorry arrangement at best; the repairs would not take too much punishment, and Jesse knew he might have to work on them again before he was done. But they were far better than no snowshoes at all, and very probably made the difference between living and dying.

Lashing up the bedroll and putting the pack in order, he worked the straps over his bulky coat and shifted the weight until it was comfortable. There was not much food left, now. Maybe enough for two days. It was not a matter of concern, since the downward trip would not take nearly as long as had the climbing. Too, there were a few cans down where he had parted company with the sorrel. Jesse doubted that he would need them, but they were there as added insurance.

Going to the door, then, and reaching for the hook, he suddenly remembered the dream—if it was a dream—and hesitated. It was so vivid in his mind: the sounds, and knowing the lion had come. He remembered starting to open the door, but nothing after that. There was no recollection of changing his mind and going back to the bedroll, and yet in his bedroll was where the day had found him. A dream . . . Jesse took a breath. Yes, it made no sense otherwise.

Opening the door, he found the snow reaching more than four feet above the level of the floor. It would mean half climbing and half digging his way out, but he remembered that the window was on a more sheltered side of the cabin, and chose it to make his exit. Once outside, Jesse put the snowshoes on and worked his way around to the front.

If he had ever worn such things, when he was small, the experience was lost to him. And they were awkward. Jesse stepped away from the cabin and across the snow with all the grace of a fat, barnyard duck.

Perhaps one grew accustomed to them, but he could not imagine it. He was so preoccupied with the task of moving, without one shoe stepping on the other, that at first he was not aware of the tracks punched in that fresh, powdery surface. Without comprehension, Jesse saw them—and then stopped. The lion *had* come to him.

With a sudden chill deeper than that wintry air, he turned and saw that the tracks approached to within maybe twenty feet of the cabin before doubling back. The big cat could not have scratched at the door. The sounds he had heard must have been part of the wind.

Jesse went back to the cabin, and from near the doorway, tried to make sense of it. If the lion had followed him here in the storm, that would have been one thing. It would have been reasonable, because the creature had followed him once before, and what happened last night could be written off as a dream and forgotten. But if that had been the case, its tracks would have been filled in and covered over.

It occurred to him, then, that the lion could have come just a short while ago. Perhaps it had smelled smoke and the meat he was cooking. The notion made a lot of sense, until he squatted down and made a closer examination of the tracks. Reaching into the holes, he found that the snow was not packed but still powder; they were only about half of their original depth. And the discovery put him right back where he had started. It could not be avoided: The lion had come during the last of the storm.

But the noises—and knowing it had come—Jesse was still not convinced that he had gotten up last night. No matter how he looked at it, there was that matter of remembering absolutely nothing beyond the moment of reaching for the latch hook. And if nothing else, he could not imagine himself wanting to open the door under those circumstances. The whole episode had all the earmarks of a dream. And yet, here were the tracks! Dream and fact had come together, and the implications were both bewildering and frightening.

Was it a coincidence, dreaming of the lion at a time when it was actually there? Or was the lion some kind of spirit, so intense in nature that it could reach inside and touch a sleeping mind?

No matter how difficult it was to accept, it had to be a coincidence. The second question was too disturbing; it had to be dropped and avoided. But with this fresh assault on his senses, all his earlier intentions were left hanging and in doubt. The storm was over, and it had not, as anticipated, deprived him of tracks to follow. Where was there a reason, now, for heading downward and out of the snow? The snow itself? It was hard to get used to the idea, but the snow was no longer a deciding factor. As long as the shoes held together, the depth of the drifts did not matter. And there was food enough for a couple of days . . . longer, if he was careful.

On the other hand, sundown was not many hours away; night would come again. How far could he go before he was compelled to stop and prepare himself for the dark's long and searing cold? And how far away was the lion? The tracks were not proof that it was not already well out of reach. To continue with the hunt, then, was very probably foolish and pointless. But, faced with it, Jesse still was not able to leave the mountain. Not yet. The tracks had to be followed, just one more time.

The lion's trace returned, eventually, to the half-buried carcass of the deer. Part of it, now, had been eaten. From there, the tracks almost doubled back on themselves, bending a little to the northeast. And they seemed fresher. Jesse supposed he had narrowed the distance considerably while the lion was eating. But he also wondered, now that he was accustomed to the snow-shoes, if he was not able to travel faster than the lion. There were places, windblown, where relatively little snow had accumulated. But in most areas, the new powder was at least three feet deep and probably as much as ten in the drifts. The lion would be plunging in up to its belly much of the time.

That he was, indeed, moving faster than the cat became strikingly apparent less than an hour beyond the deer's carcass. He found the top edges of the tracks still crumbling. Jesse took it as a warning and stopped. Squatting down on his heels, he studied the region ahead—the wide expanses of open snow and the clustering spikes of trees, and even that raw, towering mass of granite that rose far above the timberline and disappeared in the clouds. And nothing moved out there; certainly there was nothing to hear. But the lion had to be somewhere close, maybe only minutes away.

For another quarter of an hour, he hurried after his quarry, expecting with each passing minute to finally catch sight of it. His lungs burned with each gasp of that cold air; his breathing sounded to him like explosions against the mountain's silence. But it availed him nothing. He was close, but not close enough. And time was running out.

He was not aware of the hour until the ridge turned red, and the red spread quickly upward to catch the steep walls of that high tower. To the west, the clouds were catching fire. It portended clear weather . . . clear, and probably colder than it would have been, where he was. But the immediate problem was that the sun was going down. Little time remained for him to prepare for the night. He should have stopped an hour ago.

Jesse quickly headed down into a dense stand of timber, found a level place for a camp, and immediately began gathering wood. He collected it in the outlying sections of the stand first. That way, when darkness came and he built a fire, he would not have to go more than a few yards from camp to find more.

And it was not bad when he finally settled down. There was very little wind to steal the heat this time. And as long as he slept lightly enough to get up now and then to keep the fire going, he would stay reasonably warm. It was far better than had been expected. But the lion—Jesse did not think it would come to him again. Ever since feeding on the deer, it had given the impression of trying to get away. And he had come so close.

Resting and close to sleep, he begged and prayed that the lion would also rest and still be close by in the morning.

Somewhere around midnight, Jesse woke up and could not sleep again. Above, between the trees, he saw bright stars wheeling . . . the clouds were gone already. And he realized that the starlight, combined with that almost spectral glow of the snow, was sufficient for seeing. The idea would not leave him alone; he was too restless. Maybe the lion was too accustomed to his habits. Yes, and if he moved unexpectedly. . . .

Jesse rested for another hour and then made coffee. When he was fully awake and warmed, he broke camp and slowly followed the tracks toward morning.

16.

The night and that mountain were made of crystal and silver. And the air, the cold and silence of it, was sharply brittle; a sudden cracking sound might have shattered the sky and sent the stars powdering down. To Jesse, it could have been wondered if, in all that vastness and deep, time both began and ended. Morning seemed unlikely.

There were times during the night when the tracks passed into timbered shadow and he lost them. But they were always there again, beyond the dark and cutting across those open expanses of snow.

If made of crystal and silver, it was also a dead world . . . or the profound sleep of mountains. It was the nature of darkened wilderness to seem empty, given the conspiracy of winter's lingering specter. But the effect was almost hypnotic: There were no quick flights of birds, no bright dances of butterflies, and no small creatures scurrying away at his approach. The night did not even have enough air to make the trees move. Jesse knew only the steam his breath made, and the creaking whisper of his snowshoes. With nothing else to feed his attention, he found himself too easily going blank . . .

following the tracks, but not remaining alert to what the distance ahead might reveal.

The only way Jesse could deal with the problem was to force himself to look far ahead, and make a game of it. In five minutes, he told himself, he would see the lion leaving a stand of trees and crossing the snow. Under his breath, he counted off the seconds and watched the trees very carefully. The lion did not appear at the magic moment, of course; he had to give it another five minutes and start the count all over again. And it worked reasonably well. But now and then, he still found himself staring down at the webbing of his snowshoes.

And the question of what those blind intervals might have held was disturbing.

When the eastern stars began to falter and grow dim, and dawn came to the edge of the universe, the tracks turned downward for a short distance. They led Jesse to a place of pine and stone—a hollow, beneath a protecting bluff, that had escaped the snow.

Here, he suspected, the lion had rested. The earth was softly carpeted with needles and seemed to have been disturbed. His hands were too cold for him to trust what he felt, but pressing his palms into the needles, Jesse sensed a remaining warmth . . . or a lesser cold. He could not even begin to be sure about it.

But if the lion had stopped here, why had it left in the dark and so soon after traveling most of the night? Perhaps it had known he was coming: a warning scent in that cold air, the sound of his snowshoes carrying too far in mountain stillness. And, naturally, since the tracks had been so easily followed through the night, he himself had been anything but invisible.

It was defeating. How many times had he come close enough to interrupt the lion, to disturb it into hurrying away; how many times without a chance for a shot or even catching a glimpse of his target? But there was nothing he could do about the noise, or the scent, or his visibility—not and still stay with the tracks or keep pace with the lion. Once again, Jesse wondered if there was any point in trying to hunt a lion without dogs—good hounds to put the cat up a tree and keep it there.

But it was not the time for making excuses, no matter how justified they were. He had not come that far to throw away what little chance or advantage he might have gained. If it was true that he had felt warmth with his hands, then it was also true that warmth would be short-lived in that icy air; and how far away could the lion have gone in that time?

Jesse followed the trace upward again, and regaining the ridge, discovered that they were continuing to climb, abandoning the mountain's shoulder and the last of shielding timber, and reaching with awesome certainty for that final and towering fortress. He had never thought or dreamed that the hunt would take him into those forbidding reaches, but he regarded the reality of it with a confused mixture of shock, dismay, and a growing curiosity.

This sudden departure from what had seemed reasonable and expected was the best evidence yet, perhaps, that the lion knew very well of his continuing pursuit. But that disturbing question came again: Was the animal going to an extreme in one last effort to escape? Or was it trying to draw him in to some awkward and precarious place where, with four-footed sureness, it could better deal with him?

Jesse tried to think as the lion would. But how? Perhaps the lion knew this part of the world, or at least could depend on its instincts. But what could he do about it? Nothing, except keep his eyes open. . . .

Not wanting the weight, or any restriction of his ability to move, he got rid of the pack. Putting it on top of a rock where it could easily be seen, and marking the spot in his mind, Jesse began the final climb. Perhaps that tower reached high enough to know an everlasting wind. Close to its base, now, and looking almost straight up, he could see ghosts, plumes of snow blowing out into the growing blue of the sky . . . and he could hear it, too, a far thin roaring that made the mountain seem alive. It was eerie. . . .

And somewhere above him, the lion—or demon. The way the earth rose and ended there, with bleak rock and the voice of gales, was all too suitable for what had been thought of as a marauding spirit.

Jesse did not hesitate. But it was as if more than his own legs and will compelled him to climb. With each step, something warned him to go back. All he could see, in his mind, was a man . . . his father who, having emptied a rifle at darkness, hurried back into the house to lock the door as if against some black thing . . . collapsing in a chair to shake, staring and listening to God knows what . . . and refusing, until daylight, to let himself sleep. Demon, force of evil . . . as if that mountain itself were some kind of spirit that attacked the last of reason, Jesse was no longer certain of what he followed.

Within the space of a few minutes, the spell of that place deepened and took on a new strangeness. It seemed to be no more than a wind at first, an element scarcely worth his attention. And it was just a wind, in that it made the trees below him sway and sing with their usual and gentle music. But in some way it was different, and the difference was so simple, so unexpectedly obvious that it took a while to realize exactly what it was.

The wind was *warm* . . . and the sun had yet to rise.

17.

The wind was called chinook, and when its warmth slowly collided with bitter air and snow, and those high, wintered masses of stone, a thick fog formed to hide the rising sun. It moved, an earth-clinging cloud, and brought softness to the morning. But there was no seeing in it. Rocks that were only a few yards away quietly dissolved and ceased to exist.

Jesse removed the snowshoes and leaned them against a rock for later. Very little snow had stuck to the south face of the massif, and the shoes would have only been a hindrance. But before continuing, he tried to appraise the situation. He was accustomed to San Francisco fog, the way it came rolling through the Gate in the evenings. It was a gentle thing and smelled of salt, and was sometimes thick enough to wisp around the streetlights at night. But what the wind made here was beyond his experience, and it held a certain danger.

He was not afraid of becoming lost; in following the lion up those first ramparts of the tower, he found only one place to climb: a serpentine path that was little more than a ledge at times. And even if there had been other routes to confuse his way, Jesse did not expect the fog to endure far into the morning. The sun would burn it off, eventually. Neither was he afraid of falling. As long as he could see a few paces ahead, and moved slowly, there would be ample warning of any sudden dropoffs.

But in that drifting gray, he could be too close to the lion and not have the slightest hint of its presence. If the big cat, even now, was only trying to get away, the only risk involved was that of missing a chance to shoot. And, of course, it would be easy in that fog for the lion to jump onto some boulder above the path, and wait for him to go on by . . . letting him continue to climb, while it went back down.

If, however, that devil was trying to lure him into a bad spot where it could attack, then the fog was much to its advantage. Invisible until the very last instant, it could be on him before he even had a chance to move.

Jesse thought of simply staying where he was and waiting for the fog to lift. But he could not look around him and say that it was a safe place to be. There were no safe places; not while visibility was so limited. And he considered turning back and going down, but even retreat offered no guarantees. The fog would exist wherever there was snow to generate it, and the lion could follow.

It would have been pointless, then, not to go on. Keeping the rifle up and ready to fire, as much as climbing would permit, Jesse moved through the fog and tried to be as quiet as the lion. He knew that, no matter how slowly and quietly he went, his scent would betray him. But he did not want his boots or the rustle of clothing to mask whatever sound the lion might make. And what little he could see, he wanted time to see carefully.

Just as had been his experience earlier, in the dark, in the rain, and also in the blizzard, he had difficulty with common, inanimate objects around him. Dimmed and diffused by wisping currents of fog, boulders assumed odd shapes; patches of gravel and snow slowly emerged in strange patterns. And like a frightened child who thought shadows were real, Jesse jumped at them and found himself moving slower still. He knew perfectly well what was happening: Expecting a lion, his mind fashioned lions from innocent stone. But there were no promises, no assurances that, among those granite phantoms, there would not be one to breathe, and move, and suddenly charge with a terrifying fury; and the tension of it was heavy, a thing that knotted along his muscles and brought beads of sweat to his face.

Jesse did not know how long or how far he climbed. An hour. Perhaps two. And still taking one careful step at a time, he probably covered less than half a mile.

The broken jumble of boulders on his left slowly gave way to a high and unbroken wall of stone, and the path narrowed down to become and remain a ledge. As long as it did not grow any smaller, there would be no difficulty in climbing. But beyond the ledge, and obscured by the fog, was a drop of an unknown angle and depth. And the idea of being that close to empty space, especially when he could not see the extent of it, was not to his liking.

If the lion had intended to draw him into a place where he had little room for maneuvering, then it had succeeded. But, in other ways, Jesse also felt that he was better off than before. By pressing close to the wall, he reduced the danger of being attacked from above. And unless the demon had wings, there was no chance of it jumping him from the right. In front of, and behind him: Those were the only directions he really had to worry about.

After a few minutes more, the fog showed signs of thinning. It was not apparent, at first, whether he was climbing out of it or if the sunlight had turned warm enough to finally start burning it off. But a brightness came to it, and above him there was a hint of blue. Glistening patches of rock and snow appeared at greater distances. And then, as quickly as it took him to step a dozen paces, the fog lifted away and was gone.

After so long in a subdued light, Jesse was not ready for the sun's brightness. In that thin air, its rays were so intense that, for a few painful moments, he was almost blind. Only vaguely aware of the deep drop that yawned to his right, he squinted and shielded his eyes, and continued around a turn.

And lion or spirit, it was suddenly there, waiting for him.

18.

The thing was too close. Terrified and filled with the impulse to turn and run, Jesse stumbled and grabbed at stone to keep himself from falling. And there, as if the time for escaping had been lost, he froze. Before him, dark and almost hidden in the fire of the sun, was a creature that appeared to be all that had been suspected and imagined of it; immortal smoke, a vaporous image of coiling muscles and fury; only the eyes seemed real, a hard, blazing yellow. And at his right, now only inches from his boot, a sheer drop of perhaps eighty or ninety feet. His startled senses divided and overwhelmed, he sucked air into his lungs and jammed his eyes shut.

For those few seconds of frightened questioning, Jesse did not know what to do. It seemed obvious that, in spite of having warned himself of the possibility, he had been drawn into a position where the lion had the advantage. *Lion?* His fingers tightened around the rifle, and he wondered if it was not useless. He had seen the lion, now, and remembered his father and the Ferguses . . . Joe had tried to tell him . . . and the rifle had failed before, at almost point-blank range.

What else could he do except try to get away from

there? Maybe, Jesse told himself, if he backed off an inch at a time, that thing would stay where it was and not follow. Taking another deep breath, he forced his eyes open and started to move backward—and then hesitated. With time and a second look, the fact of the precipice had begun to settle in his mind; that first, startled impression had passed.

And the lion had not moved, but still crouched there, maybe twenty feet away. What was it waiting for? Rather than stand there, like a tempting bit of bait, Jesse took a slow step back. But as he moved, so did the lion; ears flattened, it came up on its legs and seemed on the verge of exploding across that short distance.

Jesse held still, not even breathing. The devil apparently was not about to bargain. However useless it might again prove to be, the rifle was his only alternative. Without looking down, he pulled the hammer back with his thumb. And for that moment, he remembered how, once, the sound of a rifle alone was enough to drive it away from sheep and back across the fence . . . and maybe the same had been true, later, in that outcropping of stone. The next day, at least, found the lion still climbing. But somehow he knew it was different here. Maybe this bleak place beneath a wind-roaring summit was home to a spirit and had to be defended.

Forcing himself to do it slowly, Jesse raised the carbine and aimed at a point between gleaming eyes. His finger tightened on the trigger . . . and eased off again. Perhaps his eyes had grown accustomed to the brightness, and maybe the sun had climbed enough to be less direct . . . but the image, what he had come to think, the whole idea . . . all of it began to crumble.

Strangely, the first thing that came into changing awareness was the fact that, beyond the creature, the ledge failed completely for ten or twelve feet. And how could something with the substance of smoke be cornered? With that, his attention returned to the eyes—not pools of hellfire, but simply eyes full of anger and maybe even fear—eyes that blinked and were pale with the milkiness of beginning cataracts. Looking past the eyes, Jesse realized that the demon had hunger's protruding ribs, and a coat that was dull, patchy, and marked with too many scars.

He lowered the rifle an inch or two, dismayed and beginning to understand. Demon, force of evil . . . merely a lion. It was obvious, even to one who had been away and raised in a city, that the animal was different only in that it had lived longer than, perhaps, nature intended.

In that instant of recognition, so much began to make sense. If his father and Charlie Fergus had ever seen the lion, they could not have failed to understand. But all they had known was a boldness that exceeded the normal patterns. With the truth hidden, its cunning seemed supernatural. And yet it was nothing more than the courage and artfulness that came of having grown too old to hunt in the usual way. Its only motive was to survive, and what choice did it have but to haunt man's back fences and prey on clumsy livestock? That sick, half-dead deer . . . for the lion to have found anything as easily taken as that could hardly have been more than a rare accident. And the dead sheep . . . perhaps the hunt had prevented it from coming back to claim its kill. But it seemed more likely that his father's practice of firing the rifle from the back porch had, for too long a time, kept the lion from eating. Looking at that dismal beast, Jesse could not imagine it being able to climb over the gate with a full-grown sheep.

Still, here and now, the lion was a considerable danger to be reckoned with. Indeed, all considered, the danger was probably intensified. A younger lion would have been willing and able to leap across the gap to where the ledge began again. But this animal had run out of choices. Ready to fight, it measured him as surely as he measured it, and so that moment was extremely delicate and volatile.

Jesse aimed the rifle again . . . and still could not shoot. Why? It was right there, and he could not miss. Why could he not pull the trigger and put an end to an old and troublesome marauder? It would even be a kindness, if death was kind. But he had never shot an animal before, and did not know how . . . not just like that. The mechanics of it were simple, merely the squeezing of a trigger, but the idea of it was something else . . . the ending of a life. Kindness? He wondered if he had the right to make that kind of judgment.

Almost angrily, he wished the lion would at least try to make the jump across the gap. It would escape, if it did; he could not follow.

Jesse decided to try backing off again. Maybe the lion would permit it, this time. But when he lowered the rifle all the way, and moved his leg, the motion apparently startled the lion. It unleashed its coiled muscles and leaped at him with a scream exploding from its throat.

It happened much too fast for Jesse to react and get the rifle up again. And the distance was too short, anyway; the lion's flying body, dead or alive, would have knocked him off the ledge. And so he dived for the ledge; fell, sprawled, trying to get down and out of the way. Some part of the lion slammed across his back, and at the same time, he lost his grip on the rifle and heard it clattering somewhere far below.

Close to panic at having no way to defend himself, Jesse scrambled to his feet and turned to face the lion . . . and it was gone. At first, he thought that the lion had just continued along the ledge, its momentum having carried it around the bend. And after waiting a minute, with no sign of its returning, he began to believe that the lion had kept on going to make good its escape.

But, beginning to breathe more easily, he looked down to see where the rifle had fallen—and saw the cat, a broken thing, on the rocks below.

19.

Jesse was too startled by that unexpected turn of events to do anything but stand there and stare. It was over—the nightmare that had prowled the slopes of home. The long hunt had come to an end. And the fact of it refused to settle in his mind, as if at any moment, now, the lion might move . . . might breathe and stir, and with a defiant lashing of its tail, go down again to timberline and invisibility.

It had happened in such an unexpected way, and in a sense, too easily. After all those days and nights, hunter and lion locked in a relentless climb to the high country—even after surviving a blizzard, and continuing upward into the last of the world—after all that, and finally confronting each other. Well, he had not been mangled by teeth and claws, and the lion had not been stilled by a last-chance bullet through its vitals. No, he had only skinned his knees a little, and the lion was sprawled across brutal rock . . . dead of a *fall.*

But when the surprise of it began to fade, Jesse knew a confusion of feelings. Part of it was anger, and for a moment he thought of the lion as having been no more than a dumb animal; dumb for attacking him when he was clearly making every effort to back away and leave it alone. And out of anger came a sensation of triumph and accomplishment. Fresh from the city and completely inexperienced, he had nevertheless taken it upon himself to rid his father and the Ferguses of a marauder that had dominated their lives and land—something they had not been able to do themselves—and regardless of how it happened, he had succeeded.

And yet, anger and triumph neither sat well nor lasted for long. Looking down at the lion, and seeing again its age, its scars, the protruding ribs, Jesse became too aware of having been involved in the death of a creature that had only tried to live. And with this came an inestimable sadness.

To his father and the others, the cat had been one thing; to himself, it had been something else—something he had known, really, only in the last minute of its life. And it *was* a marauder, a killer, and in some sense of the word even demonic in its furious efforts to survive. But evil? No . . . only an inconvenience in that men and lion had tried to live off the same stretch of land. Were it not for hunger and the accident of its age, the big cat would never have come to them. And he would not have hunted it, and it would be alive and strong, wandering in the secrecy of its own mountains.

Jesse turned away, and leaning against stone, began to weep.

20.

There was neither heart nor courage in him to find a way down to the rifle his father had given him so long ago. Very probably it had been damaged, its barrel perhaps no longer true, but Jesse had thought only that he did not want to look at the lion again.

It was best to forget, or at least to understand. And there *was* a small, faltering thing at the edge of his mind that tried to tell him how quickly the lion had died . . . how much easier it was than the slow death of sickness and starvation. But it would be a long time before he was far enough away from that day to let it fade, or to finally know its truth.

And so, after a while, Jesse simply turned and went back along what had been pursuit's vengeful and frightening path, down along widening ledge and into afternoon, stopping only to retrieve the snowshoes. Not once did he look back at that high, jagged tower and its plumes of wind-driven snow, and neither did he listen to its voice. Getting down and away from those mountains —and maybe going back to San Francisco now—they were all he could think of.

When he reached his pack, he could not help noticing

how warm the day had become. Warm and clear, and
the earth seeming to stir with it. Spring, perhaps, had
finally returned to those high places.

Jesse stopped, not far from the cabin, to build a fire
and cook a meal. There was no thought, at first, of staying and making use of its shelter again. The night would
be clear, full of stars for seeing, and warmer than before,
and he had planned to just keep on going. If he could
put the snow behind him before sunrise, he knew it might
be possible to reach the house by tomorrow night. Maybe
sooner . . . once free of the snowshoes, and traveling
downhill most of the time, he could cover the miles
quickly.

But for part of a night and most of that day he had
already climbed too much and gone too far; the lion's
death had taken a lot out of him. And the food did the
rest. Exhausted, barely able to keep his eyes open, Jesse
killed the fire and made his way down to the cabin. He
did not wait for the sun to go down, or spend time remembering the storm and how this place had saved his
life. Spreading the bedroll on the floor, he got out of his
clothes and crawled into the blankets to fall instantly
asleep.

And somewhere in the night that came, he dreamed
again of the lion. It had come to the cabin once more,
not in a storm as before, and not to scream and scratch
at the door. The snow was gone, and the lion sat for a
while on soft, carpeted earth and washed itself. Its scars
were gone and its eyes were clear, and its ribs were hidden beneath the fat of good hunting. And when it was

done washing, it looked toward the cabin for a moment, and then peacefully walked away.

Jesse woke with a start and hurried to open the door, wondering. . . .

He was able to discard the snowshoes at midmorning. Light-footed and almost at a run, he hurried down toward the distant valley and the slopes of home. Jesse wanted a hot bath that evening, a shave and a change of clothes . . . and then maybe he would ride the sorrel over to the Ferguses. He would tell them about the lion, and it would be good to hear human voices again. There was something else to learn, but he did not want to think about it; not yet.

But he lost the race with the sun, and night came again. Jesse was not too tired to go on. Indeed, he tried for a while. It was just that, without snow to catch the stars, he could not see the way. And so it meant one more camp, and cooking one more meal, and sleeping fitfully until, at last, that long night began to fade.

Jesse felt the first warm rays of the sun on his back when he reached the last of those lesser ridges and saw the house below, still sleeping in the shadows of the mountains. It was a welcome sight; a hard journey was nearly over. But it was also a disturbing thing. The unmoving quiet around that house was too full of unhappy implications.

He went not quite as quickly now. It was another half hour before he came to the back fence. Jesse climbed the gate, rather than bother with the chain. But he had no more than reached the top board, and was straddling it, when he saw something to make him stop. Looking at the house again, he saw smoke rising from the kitchen chimney. It was not the Ferguses; the Jeep was not parked in the yard. And Joe would not have stayed there alone. But somebody was cooking breakfast.

Jesse climbed down, almost falling in his haste. His father was home.

J. Allan Bosworth began writing while still a radioman aboard the U.S.S. *Missouri*. World War II had just ended, and the ship was on her long voyage home. A native of California, he returned to San Francisco and took a job at the *Chronicle*. Ten years later, having published two novels and a few dozen short stories, he left the newspaper to begin writing on a full-time basis. He and his wife and two daughters now live in Salem, Virginia. Among Mr. Bosworth's previous books for young people are *White Water, Still Water; All the Dark Places; A Wind Named Anne;* and *A Darkness of Giants.*

DA

GAYLORD   PRINTED IN U.S.A.